John Flint's
Bastard

Here's what readers are saying about "Of Chains and Slavery."

"Commander Johnson has given us an intriguing and fast-paced adventure page-turner that should be on every high schooler's required reading list; weaving together the warp of pre-revolution history with the woof of classic pirate fiction to fashion a master tapestry describing the complicated and brutal life of this new swashbuckling hero, Joshua Smoot. This novel cries out to become a major motion picture."

Doug Hawley, Owner of "Ye Landmark Collectibles" of Poulsbo, WA

"Master storyteller Roger Johnson takes us on an incredible adventure as we follow Joshua Smoot from his kidnapping from Savannah to his ultimate life as a pirate in search for the legendary Treasure of Dead Man's Chest. *"John Flint's Bastard"* has it all; high adventure, treachery, honor, gasping emotion, white-knuckled drama, all wrapped in a suspenseful story line that will not let you go. Well done, Commander Johnson!"

Robert Ceccarini, NYPD Detective Lieutenant

"An exciting adventure that transports you to another time and place. Well researched and explained. I look forward to reading more by Commander Johnson."

Joe Marek, Merrick's Privateers

"It was a genuine pleasure reading *"John Flint's Bastard."* It is an exciting blend of history and fiction during the end of the Age of Piracy and the beginning of the Age of Liberty. Make room Blackbeard, Billy the Kid, and Captain Hook, because there's a new Swashbuckler named Joshua Smoot riding the high seas."

Wade John Taylor, editor, The Pamphlet

"If you love America, you will love *"John Flint's Bastard, Slavery and Revenge,"* and the third book in this pirate adventure trilogy, *"Treasure and Redemption."* Commander Johnson spins a compelling yarn that takes place just before the American founding, and introduces us to a new swashbuckler named Joshua Smoot. A true page-turner that I could not put down. I look forward to part three."

Corey Millard, avid reader of pirate adventure

"A brilliantly painted canvas of the by-gone Golden Age of Piracy and the introduction of Joshua Smoot! Filled with intrigue, suspense, and both joyful and bitter raw emotion; Commander Johnson weaves a tale of the destiny of souls that will stir the hearts of all that read their way into this epic story! I highly recommend the trilogy!"

Penny Caldwell, author, "The God of the Mountain."

"As a child, I read and re-read Treasure Island and have hungered all these decades to learn the ultimate destination of Long John Silver and the rest of that famous treasure. That hunger has now been satisfied in Commander Johnson's trilogy, *"Of Chains and Slavery."* Written in the classic style of Robert Louis Stevenson, this fast-moving pirate novel follows the complicated life and adventures of John Flint's bastard—Joshua Smoot—from his kidnapping at Savannah, through his years as a slave, and finally to his quest for the Treasure of Dead Man's Chest. A must read for those who share my hunger."

Scott C. Kuesel, Wisconsin Maritime Historical Society

"How important is a man's identity, and what is he willing to sacrifice to keep it? These are the life-changing decisions young Joshua Smoot—the bastard son of the notorious pirate John Flint—must make. Will his odyssey break him or will he find the courage, strength, and faith to survive and conquer the life he's been forced into? The *"Of Chains and Slavery"* trilogy is a wild ride and a must read."

Michael Carver, Historical Interpreter and Reenactor

John Flint's Bastard

Of Chains and Slavery

~

A Trilogy: Part One

Roger L. Johnson
Commander, USN

SEAWORTHY PUBLICATIONS, INC. • MELBOURNE, FLORIDA

John Flint's Bastard
Of Chains and Slavery, A Trilogy: Part One
Copyright ©2025 by Roger L. Johnson
Commander, USN
ISBN: 978-1-948494-84-7
Published in the USA by:
Seaworthy Publications, Inc.
6300 N Wickham Rd.
Unit #130-416
Melbourne, FL 32940
Phone 321-389-2506
e-mail orders@seaworthy.com
www.seaworthy.com

Library of Congress Cataloging-in-Publication Data

Names: Johnson, Roger L., Commander, author.
Title: John Flint's bastard / Roger L. Johnson, Commander, U.S. Navy (retired).
Description: Melbourne, Florida : Seaworthy Publications, Inc., 2024. | Series: Of chains and slavery, a trilogy ; part 1 | Summary: "Welcome to the world of Joshua Smoot-the bastard son of Treasure Island's John Flint. From the first page of John Flint's Bastard to the last, you will experience the full spectrum of love versus hate, loyalty versus betrayal, freedom versus slavery, and the extremes of mankind's goodness and evil toward one another. The old pirate Captain John Flint-the evil benefactor of Savannah-finally spawns a manchild by one of his concubines. To fulfill the last wish of the lad's mother, Flint promises to raise Joshua as a gentleman rather than make him a pirate, and to accomplish this task, he delivers the eight-year-old lad to the Wakehurst Place Estate in southern England where Joshua's stubborn spirit forces him into an ultimatum that tests his will and eventually earns him two King's warrants for his head. During his run from the King, Joshua meets and falls in love with Rebecca Keyes-a young girl with a stronger will than his own. Their rocky relationship culminates with Rebecca being forced to make a life-and-death decision that will affect Joshua's course for the rest of his life. If you like fast-paced, white-knuckled, edge-of-seat pirate adventure novels, then take your seat at the literary dining table, pick up your knife and fork, and open to chapter one of this delicious banquet called John Flint's Bastard. And when you finish, you'll want to go back to that same bookstore and buy the second in the Of Chains and Slavery trilogy, Slavery and Revenge"-- Provided by publisher.
Identifiers: LCCN 2024015572 (print) | LCCN 2024015573 (ebook) | ISBN 9781948494847 (paperback) | ISBN 9781948494854 (epub)
Subjects: LCGFT: Action and adventure fiction. | Sea fiction. | Novels.
Classification: LCC PS3610.O3753 J64 2024 (print) | LCC PS3610.O3753 (ebook) | DDC 813/.6--dc23/eng/20240404
LC record available at https://lccn.loc.gov/2024015572
LC ebook record available at https://lccn.loc.gov/2024015573

DEDICATION

I affectionately dedicate this "Of Chains and Slavery" trilogy to my wife and soul mate, Elizabeth, who has patiently endured the many months required to research and record this epic adventure of the Pirate Captain Joshua Smoot.

TABLE OF CONTENTS

FOREWORD

Why does the United States of America still stand as the bastion of freedom and liberty in a world burdened with so much pain, oppression, and suffering? It is because there are still enough patriots who remember and appreciate the sacrifices made by our Founding Fathers, and what the words truth, honesty, courage, integrity, and patriotism mean—each of which compels us to stand proudly with one hand on our heart and with the other held outstretched toward heaven, declaring, "Give me liberty or give me death!" Those are the words of the Patriot and Statesman, Patrick Henry—words that formed the heart of his famous speech given on March 23, 1775, at the Henrico Baptist Church in Richmond, Virginia.

But where did Patrick Henry get those famous words that kindled the fires of revolution in the hearts of patriotic Americans? Ask your teachers. Ask the man or woman who represents you at our nation's capital. Few will be able to name the man who said those words, fewer will be able to quote them, and none will know what inspired them.

While researching the historical records, I discovered multiple independent sources that described in detail what happened to inspire those famous words. It is not a very nice story, for those days preceding the American Revolution were desperate and oppressive times. It is so vital to your understanding of this series of novels, that I relate to you that momentous event. It demonstrates one thing that was common to all the Founding Fathers and is sorely missing in our time—that these men whom we hold in such high esteem did not do what they did because it would bring them fame, power, or wealth but rather because it was the right thing to do—for God and country—regardless of the consequences. To a man, our Founding Fathers recognized a true foe, and they did what was necessary to defeat him.

Shortly before the first shots of the American Revolution were fired at Lexington and Concord on April 19, 1775, Patrick Henry carried the latest news from a meeting of the Committees of Correspondence in Harrisonburg, Virginia to his home in Fredericksburg. As the hour was late and both he and his horse needed rest, he stopped for the night in the small hamlet of Culpeper. All the inns and public houses were empty because the entire population was crowded into the town square to witness the cat-of-nine-tails flogging of Ezekiel McClanahan, a small 65-year-old man who had been stripped naked and chained to the whipping post. Patrick asked the local constable what the frail man had done to deserve such a severe punishment. The constable—who represented the King of England and the Governor of Virginia—explained. "This is the father of one of the dozen Baptist Preachers who insist on preaching the Gospel of Jesus Christ without the King's permission. This fellow told me that he will preach his gospel whenever and wherever it is needed, and he did not care what I did to him, because he would never bow his knee to King George. He said that the Gospel is God's business, that the King is below God, and therefore, cannot grant or deny permission for the Gospel of Jesus Christ to be preached. I am about to make an example of this obstinate man to the people of Culpeper and to those other eleven preachers who stand with his son in my jail. That is why Ezekiel McClanahan is to be flogged."

Patrick moved for a better view of the spectacle. Before the flogging began, Ezekiel McClanahan twisted about in his chains and for several minutes looked into the eyes of every person in the crowd. When he was satisfied that every person was listening, the frail little man took a large breath and spoke his last words while in the flesh. "You all know me, my son William, and the other eleven men who share his jail cell. Those men have been with you at the birth of your children. They been with you when you were sick. They are there to comfort you when your aged loved ones go to be with our Lord. For the moment, those charitable roles are reversed—for instead of me attending to you in your time of need, you will attend my departure from this life to everlasting glory. We have prayed with you in your times of need and we have led many of you to a saving knowledge and belief in our Lord and Savior Jesus Christ—the Lamb of God that took away the sin of the world." The man paused to take several breaths. "Now, behold what Mother England and her reigning son, King George III, do when a minister will not bow the knee and ask for a creature's permission to preach the Creator's Gospel of Salvation!" Then, looking upward towards heaven where his reward awaited him, Ezekiel McClanahan shouted these famous words. "Is life so dear or peace so sweet as to be purchased at the price of chains and slavery? Forbid it, Almighty God! I know not what course other men may take, but as for me, give me liberty or give me death!"

The scourging lasted for only minutes, but when the blood-stained cat-of-nine-tails was finally rinsed clean and returned to its leather bag, all the skin and flesh was ripped from the preacher's back—down to the bones of his spine and ribcage.

The next morning, Patrick Henry watched as the torn and naked body of Ezekiel McClanahan was dropped unceremoniously into an unmarked shallow grave next to the roadway. Patrick waited until the grave diggers stomped the dirt firm and walked away. Once alone, he pulled the scrap of paper from his pocket that contained the preacher's last words. Surrounded in the dawn's cold ground fog, Patrick Henry removed his hat and dropped to one knee. For the first of many times, this great patriot of the American Revolution read aloud the words that would call men of valor to arms against an oppressive King. It was upon these words that the patriots fought, died, and anointed the soil of this new republic with their blood, and the same words that launched George Washington's fledgling fleet of privateers to meet a vastly-superior enemy at sea. And it was upon these same words that men of substance dedicated their lives, their fortunes, and their honor to the cause of liberty.

These three novels are born of this same spirit. Man—be he black, brown, yellow, red, or white—when pushed to the edge, will do whatever is necessary to hold onto the God-given rights of life, liberty, and property. It is the story of the native-born patriot and Pirate Captain Joshua Smoot, and of the forces that shaped him into the unique man that he became. It is also the brief but life-changing encounter Joshua had with Simbatu—an Ethiopian Jew turned Christian—who shared the same auction block at Baracoa, Cuba. Together, these two young men from diverse backgrounds and cultures struggled for the same goal—to gain their freedom and liberty from the evil men who bought and sold them into the cruel bondage of chains and slavery.

As you travel with Joshua, you will notice that nearly everyone he encounters will refer to God. Some—like the evil John Flint and Damon Hobson—will denounce Jesus Christ, while others proclaim their faith and trust in His finished work on the cross. Life expectancy during the eighteenth century was often precarious and short for those lower in the financial and social strata. When a man and a woman fell in love, they married quickly, and likewise, when their lives were threatened, they turned to their only hope, their Savior.

I therefore present to you Joshua Smoot's amazing story—the full explanation of why he became the ruthless person he was. If you have read *The Treasure of Dead Man's Chest*, you will recognize those brief but momentous encounters Joshua had with Long John Silver and John Paul Jones. Now—in this present series—you will see a portion of that great and historical saga of cunning and profound patriotism through the eyes of Joshua Smoot and the men who served with him. As with that former novel, I have changed the names of many of my characters to coincide with Robert Louis Stevenson's classic novel, *Treasure Island*, and with the prequel to that story; A.D. Howden Smith's novel, *Porto Bello Gold*.

An interesting note for those among you who have visited Savannah. According to an Archival Research and Cultural Resources study of the Lamar Ward conducted in 2007, "The area to the west of the study, across Lamar's Creek, was eventually developed by a speculative partnership, known as the Eastern Wharf Company. According to a 1991 archaeological study of the immediate area, as the 'Company' excavated the mud-blocked creek mouth, the burned hull of a ship was removed from the entrance of Lamar's Creek. Several Spanish cannons were retrieved and donated as static displays to military bases throughout the United States." This was without a doubt John Flint's pirate ship, the brigantine *Walrus*.

PREFACE

*T*hey say that the salt content of seawater is identical to that of our blood. Maybe that explains why so many of us are drawn to the sea and the wonderful stories it has spawned over the centuries. One of those stories fascinated most of us as children and still holds a special place in our hearts. If you share my love for adventure, then perhaps, like me, you've wondered after those classic pirates; the vile-to-the-bone John Flint, his lice-infested first mate Ben Gunn, and that most famous of all pirates, the softhearted cutthroat Long John Silver. Did they really exist? And if they did, what happened to them after their legendary eighteenth-century adventure?

I was in London that summer to attend a NATO-sponsored leadership symposium for command-grade military officers. Since I had arrived early at Whitehall, three days before the first session, I had the entire weekend to collect gifts and keepsakes for my wife and three children. My elder son had asked that I do some research for a term paper he was writing, so on the free Friday before the symposium, I signed into the search room of the House of Lords Record Office in the southern section of old London.

My son's term paper was on relations between the United States and England following World War I, and he had become frustrated with the lack of information in our local libraries. My search for the raw material he needed began with the Parliamentary proceedings of December 1918, the month following the allied and central powers' signing of the armistice.

As I searched for the perfect quote by Winston Churchill, I came upon the misfiled transcript of a Royal Navy Admiralty Court of Inquiry that dealt with the loss of the British brigantine *Nancy* as it was transporting arms and ammunition from Portsmouth to the British forces garrisoned at Boston.

The cover page was embossed with the Royal Navy seal, and it was dated April 5, 1777. The knot in the thin blue ribbon that bound the neat stack of parchment was crushed in such a way that it was very probable that the transcript had not been disturbed since its writing. I was nominally curious because of its age and where I had found it, and I was about to set it aside when I noticed a notation in the margin of the fifth page. There, written in the same hand as the transcript was a strange statement. "John Manley is Joshua Smoot, the bastard son of John Flint."

That note haunted me for several years before I finally began to unravel the amazing history of Joshua Smoot and his encounter with Pirate Captain John Flint at Savannah. One hundred miles to the south of Charles Town stands the unique community of Savannah, Georgia. It is situated on the Savannah River fifteen miles inland from the Atlantic Ocean and boasts an interesting genesis. In 1732, this harsh wilderness of pine groves and mosquito swamps was granted to General James Edward Oglethorpe by King George II for the purpose of creating a settlement for England's poor and those who had been imprisoned for debt. Although its growth was slow, its morals were unusually high—one of its first regulations was the absolute prohibition against the use of rum and the importation of Negroes as slaves. The general also forbade the presence of lawyers and the practice of the Catholic religion—this fourth pro-hibition being enacted because the slave-owning Spanish in Florida were pre-dominately Catholic. His prohibition against slavery did not, however, forbid the importation of hundreds of indentured servants who, once their contracts were fulfilled, were turned out to fend for themselves in an economy dom-inated by the free labor of those still serving their bonded time. This period was marked by a harshness of weather and poor economics seldom equaled in American history. The fledgling colony of Georgia was hungry for new lead-ership when, in 1743, after nearly nine years of rule as their first governor, the general abandoned the town and returned to England. His absence created a political, economic, and moral vacuum that was rapidly filled by liquor, lawyers, slavery, and by a new despotic ruler—the ruthless pirate, Captain John Flint.

In 1751, following several bad crop years, the Trustees relinquished their charter, which allowed Georgia to revert to a Royal Colony. With this change came the introduction of slavery and the establishment of the rice culture on the marshlands below the eastern bluffs of Savannah. John Flint moved into the vacated home that Oglethorpe had built on the bluff but had never oc-cupied, having returned to England before its completion. The two-story red brick mansion boasted four massive columns across the porch. And was named High Tortuga by its new inhabitant.

Captain Flint's reputation for cruelty had infected the entire eastern sea-board. Disobedient children were kept in check by the words, "John Flint will eat your heart!" It was common knowledge that in the spring of 1739, Flint sailed the *Walrus* into Salem Harbor with the body of one of his crew killed in action. The rotting thing was sewn up tight in sail canvas and thrown down in the town square. All the townsfolk were rounded up to witness the funeral and interment. With pistols at the full cock and cutlasses drawn, Flint's crew forced the hundred and ten citizens to sing hymns, throw flowers into the open grave, and even weep for the dead pirate. When the blasphemous thing was over and the dirt was finally stomped hard over the unholy grave, John Flint was slightly displeased with the townsfolk's performance. To punish them, he set fire to the church and forced them to watch it burn to the ground. Years after the cruel incident had taken place, there was much talk of removing the dead pirate from the sacred graveyard, but none of the townsfolk could muster the courage.

For over a decade, Flint and the merchants of Savannah enjoyed a prosperous and sinful relationship. Flint provided the merchants with high-quality goods at pennies on the pound from the ships he took captive, while the merchants provided the pirate and his crew with a safe port and total immunity from the law. A thousand yards to the east of the town's bluff was a seasonal stream that provided irrigation to the rice fields through a system of pumps, dikes, and gates. John Flint owned the stream and charged the plantation owners a fee for opening and closing the gates.

In 1765, Captain John Flint died of rum-induced liver sickness. Captain Billy Bones assumed the position of captain and took the *Walrus* to sea on several raids. But in the late summer of that same year, while the *Walrus* was hauled down for repairs in the Bahamas, Bones boarded another ship and ran off to England. His intention was to hire a crew, return secretly to Spyglass Island, and retrieve the L700,000 John Flint and Captain Andrew Murray had buried there. Long John Silver and most of the *Walrus'* crew followed Billy Bones to Bristol where he was hiding with the map. Like John Flint, Bones was dying of rum poisoning. Before his death, he gave the treasure map to the lad, Jimmy Hawkins. When word reached Long John Silver that there was to be an expedition to Spyglass Island, he and the *Walrus* pirates hired onto the crew of the brig *Hispaniola*.

What you are about to read is a complicated story of hatred, raw ambition, betrayal, greed, lust, cruelty, and lost love; and how an old mate of John Flint by the name of Long John Silver was able to manipulate the lives of hundreds of patriots and pirates in his attempt to attain a King's ransom in buried treasure from a small island called Dead Man's Chest—all from the note in the margin of that Royal Navy Admiralty Court of Inquiry. If I have stretched or compressed the truth by means of journalistic elasticity, I do not apologize. It's simply what we storytellers must do. I leave you with your battle cry.

THE ARMCHAIR PIRATE
The meeker the man, the more pirate he be,
Snug in his armchair, far from the sea.
He has all the fun and none of the woes,
Masters the ladies and scuttles his foes.
His armchair's his ship and reclined his position,
as he cheats the hangman, hellfire, and perdition.

Roger L. Johnson

Commander, U.S. Navy (retired)

CHAPTER ONE:
Kidnapped

A cold and tiresome mist hung thick over the small town of Savannah and the river for which it was named. Atop the bluff that overlooked Flint's Creek a thousand yards down river and to the east from the last ward, the orphans Isaac and Aaron lay in the wet beach grass with their single longbow and three coveted hunting arrows.

Isaac was becoming frustrated with his younger brother. He pointed toward John Flint's mansion and called to the lad in a loud whisper. "It's because your ears and eyes are keener than mine! That's why!" Isaac wiped the moisture from his eyebrows and studied the yard ahead. "Look and listen again! He must still be there!"

Aaron studied the pirate's compound. "The fog is still in the way."

"But you saw him, right?"

Aaron nodded. "Aye, moving toward the mansion."

"Then, where is he?"

"I can't see him right now." Aaron pointed. "He was browsing on the fresh grass next to the fence before the fog thickened."

"Then he has to still be close."

"I'm wet and I'm cold." Aaron sniffed at the dew that dripped from his nose and then pulled a sleeve across his wet face. "We've lain in this grass long enough."

"That buck is up here someplace, and I'm going to kill him."

"What—to prove that you're a man or something?"

"I'm ten years old. All the other boys my age have killed a deer, and this is my chance to prove myself."

A gust blew up and over the east-facing bluff and past the south side of the compound, disturbing the fog for a moment. Aaron's quick eye caught a movement from behind the picket fence near the side of the first out building. He pointed and whispered. "There he is!"

"Where?" Isaac wiped at his eyes and blinked quickly. "I don't see him."

"There, by that nearest corner, just inside the fence. He's eating Flint's roses. He's trapped."

"He isn't trapped." Isaac selected his favorite arrow and placed the knock at the worn spot on the bow string. "That deer leaped the fence to get in and he'll leap it again when he's ready to leave. But not if my arrow—"

"But he's inside Flint's compound. That makes him Flint's deer."

"He's nobody's deer." Isaac pulled a knee up and under his chest and then raised his body just high enough to turn the bow vertical for the shot. "Once I kill him and we drag him out of the yard, he'll be our deer." With a grunt, Isaac pulled the arrow back to his cheek, held his breath, took careful aim, and released. The snap of the string and the whistle of the twirling goose feathers reached the deer a half-second ahead of the shaft. Before the buck could rise from the lush roses to turn an ear toward the sound of approaching death, the arrow had crossed the fifty feet to its mark—a place slightly behind the shoulder blade and through the ribs to the animal's quickly beating heart. The buck jumped only once, staggered forward several steps, and collapsed backwards to the ground.

Isaac leaped to his feet with a war cry and ran forward to the fence. He stopped and turned back to Aaron. "Have you ever seen a truer shot than that?"

Aaron followed, but when he reached the fence he stopped, turned, and walked north toward the river.

Isaac watched his younger brother for a moment. "What's the matter with you?" He followed for a few paces. "I need help with the buck."

"Hush!" Aaron held up a hand to silence his older brother while he cupped the other to his ear.

"What is it? What do you hear?"

"You don't hear that?" Aaron walked past John Flint's front porch and out to the edge of the bluff.

"Hear what?" Isaac looked north toward the river and then back to Aaron. "What do you hear?"

"Shhh! Listen!" Aaron stood stone still with both his hands cupped to his ears.

Isaac stepped to his little brother's side and looked out into the fog. "You're scaring me, little brother."

Aaron pointed to a dark form slightly to their right. "There! It's a ship with bare yards and oars, pulling against the current. I knew I heard sweeps in their locks."

"I still don't..."

Before the ten-year-old boy could finish his words, a booming and vicious voice cut through the wet morning fog, up the bluff, and swept over the young boys. "Mister Gunn! Fetch aft me tankard an' a fresh cask o' rum!"

"Lord preserve us!" Aaron stepped back, as if the pirates could see him and his older brother through the fog. "It's John Flint. I told you we should not have killed his deer. He knows. He's come for us, Isaac."

Isaac dropped his bow and other two arrows in the wet grass and grabbed his younger brother by the shirt. "We have to warn the town!" He pulled his little brother through the grass toward town. "Run, Aaron! Run for your life!"

Aaron pulled loose and pointed back. "What about the deer and your arrow?"

"Leave it. We don't have time."

"But Flint will see it—the pattern of your fletching. He'll know it was us."

Isaac looked back to the rose garden. "You're right!" He ran back, grabbed up the bow and two arrows, and held them out to his brother. "Here. Hold these while I get my arrow." In a moment, Isaac was over the picket fence, the arrow was wrenched from the creature's heart, and then the two young boys ran at full speed along the north bluff toward town several hundred yards to the west. A short distance past the garrison, they ran past the edge of the three-sided wall that protected the town from land invaders, and then turned down the first street where there would be grown-ups.

Several shop owners had gathered to greet one another when the two frightened boys ran around the corner from East Bay onto Abercorn Street. The men turned one by one while the two boys passed, yelling their warning shouts of impending death.

"He's back!" It was Isaac doing most of the screaming. "John Flint has returned to eat our hearts!"

A short man in black stepped from one of the doorways. "You...Isaac and Aaron Attucks!" The sign over his head read, DAMON HOBSON – CONSTABLE & KING'S SOLICITOR. He was the first of the dreaded lawyers to invade the coastal town of Savannah, and at just over thirteen hands tall, he was a man of unapologetic cruelty. Most agreed that the little man believed that his mistreatment of those subject to his ill temperament somehow added inches to his diminutive stature. "You two!" Hobson pointed down at a spot on the walkway. "Over here! Now!"

The boys stopped and looked at each other.

"I gave you an order!" The little man gave a quick glance of superiority at the gathered shop owners. They retreated slightly. He looked back at the frightened boys. "Come here!"

Aaron followed his bigger brother across the tabby street where they stopped and looked at the man. Isaac pointed back toward the northeast. "It's true, Mister Hobson. We were up on the bluff near High Tortuga. We heard him through the fog—passing his creek. He was ordering Ben Gunn to bring him his tankard and a fresh cask o' rum."

"What were you doing on Flint's Bluff?"

"We were…" Isaac realized that he was still holding the bloody arrow. He moved it behind his back.

Aaron stepped in front of his older brother. "We were on the East Bluff gathering flowers for our Mum."

"I see no flowers, but I see a bloody arrow!" Hobson pushed Aaron aside and held out his hand. "The arrow! Give it to me!" Isaac handed the arrow to the man. "Just as I suspected." With a quick look to the other shop owners, he gave the arrow a sniff. "This is the blood of a deer." He scowled at Isaac. "You shot one of John Flint's deer, didn't you?"

Isaac turned and looked at Aaron. The younger boy gave a pained look and touched his heart while mouthing the silent words. "I told you."

"What's this malarkey you were yelling about John Flint going to eat your hearts?"

"It's true, sir." Aaron looking up at the sinister man. "He eats hearts, and everybody knows what he did to the people in Salem."

"And what, pray tell, is John Flint supposed to have done up in Salem?"

"You don't know?" Isaac studied the man as if he were daft.

Hobson gave a low growl. "I'm a friend of John Flint, and I don't like people who tell lies about him." He grabbed Isaac by the hair, dragged him forward onto the boardwalk, and gave him a rough shake. "What is it that everybody knows about my friend, Captain Flint?"

"They buried that rotting pirate's corps right in the middle of the church graveyard between the dead Vicar and his wife! Then Flint burned down the church and forced the town folk to watch!"

"Who told you that rot?"

"It's a common tale—"

Hobson gave the boy's hair another vicious jerk to silence him.

"The lad's right, Hobson!" It was the smithy. He walked past the others and across the street to the lawyer. "My brother was there. Flint killed one of the women for refusing to weep over the grave. They cut out her heart, cooked it over the fire, and John Flint ate it in front of everybody!" The blacksmith grabbed Hobson's forearm and gave it a vice-like squeeze while he pulled the boy from the constable's grip. "Release the lad or I'll break your arm, Mister Hobson!"

The little man winced at the iron grip and opened his hand. Isaac scrambled away to his brother.

"John Flint may bring us the spoils of his dark trade, but as God is my witness, I hate the man and everything he stands for!"

Hobson looked around at the other angry men and then backed toward his doorway. "You say that now, but I know every one of you will be at the docks to buy the spoils of his pirating—whatever you can afford."

The little man was right. Before the massive ship's first hawser could be thrown across to the Cotton Docks, the other merchants had already come from their shops to begin bidding for the piles of Spanish booty strewn across the main deck and that filled the ship's great hold.

Captain John Flint was a frightening site, with a dark reputation that matched his appearance. He was an exceptionally tall man at just over nineteen hands, with deep set eyes, heavy black brows, a hawkish Roman nose, an open wound for a mouth, and his tar-black hair drawn back in a tight queue. Life at sea had been brutal on the man, leaving his face the color of stained leather. Although clean shaven, the thick stubble gave his cheeks and upper lip a tinge of blue, as if permanently stained by indigo. His words were few, severe, and never challenged by those who cherished their lives. Even the sound of his name sent a chill down their spines.

The *Walrus* was pulled sideways to the docks with John Flint standing high on the quarterdeck, his blue waistcoat dripping from the heavy mist. He surveyed the town that stood on the bluff above the river with disdain. He raised his customary tankard and took a full mouth of undiluted Jamaican rum. Benjamin Gunn, Flints first mate, stood at his lee side with a small wooden cask to keep the tankard full. Gunn was a thin and nervous man a year younger than Flint. The two had indentured themselves to the plantations of Jamaica in '32 and had been inseparable since their release.

On the main deck stood several great mounds of Spanish plunder. The *Walrus*'s powder monkeys stood atop the piles and called to the crowd while holding up bolts of fine English linen, lady's hats and shoes, and various pieces of cookware. There were bone China serving sets, embroidered table linens, and jewelry of gold and silver set with expensive stones. There were also bolts of plaid from Scotland, and toward the bow stood ten bundles of whale baleen that would eventually be trimmed and used in the women's corsets. There were also twenty Negro slaves chained neck to neck and standing in a circle around eight large casks of rum.

Flint watched with mild detachment while the gangway was hoisted out, locked in place, and lowered to the dock. Before the merchants could swarm aboard, a small man in black pushed his way through the press and onto the ship. He marched across the main deck, stopped beneath John Flint, and squinted up through the mist.

Flint pretended to not see the little man at first, but then with careful aim, threw the last inch of rum in his direction. "Back again, Mister Hobson?"

The man dodged most of the cascading rum and called back above the noise of the merchants. "I found another one of your bastards, and this one is a boy!"

"Truly?" Flint threw his tankard aside, gripped the rail, and looked down at the little man. "Or are you just hungry for the thirty Spanish dollars I offered?"

"I can take you there now!"

Flint turned, gave two of his crew a rough shove, and marched down the starboard ladder to the main deck. Ben Gunn followed at several paces, bumping into his captain as Flint stopped and looked at the barrels of rum next to the main mast. He searched the eager faces of the merchants and then pointed at an overweight man who was just then stepping off the gangway onto the deck. He wore the distinctive apron of his trade. "You there—Innkeeper!" Flint pointed. "Do you want that rum?"

"Aye, if I can afford it." The man pulled his purse from his pocket and gave it a shake.

Flint licked his lips as he guessed at the sound. "My price is ten dollars each."

The man emptied the various coins into his right hand and held them out to the pirate. "I have enough for three of them."

Flint took the money and turned to a crewman with a peg leg. "John Silver! I'll be gone for a glass. Keep the prices high, and don't lower them until the merchants run out of money."

"So, you want the *Walrus* kept here for two days like always?"

"Aye, but things might change."

"Oh?"

Flint pointed at the constable. "Damon Hobson claims I have a son. What we do next depends on what this carbuncle of a man has to show me."

Hobson stepped close and touched Flint's hand. "You promised me thirty Spanish dollars if I found your bastard son."

Flint recoiled at the small man's smell—a combination of rotting flesh and camphor. The pirate gave the man an angry look and brushed past him toward the gangway.

"Don't worry, Hobson." It was Ben Gunn. "John Flint pays his debts but never 'till he's satisfied with the goods." Ben turned and followed his master down to the dock. Without a word, the crewmen and merchants stepped aside and tipped their hats in respect to the passing captain of pirates. By the time Hobson had caught up, Flint was seated in his single horse black carriage.

Flint growled. "Are you certain this time?"

"Yes, and I have the proof." Hobson climbed up to his seat, turned the carriage about, and laid the whip to the young gelding's back. Obediently, the horse trotted across the oak planks that formed the dock, onto the rough ballast stone roadway, and the slight hill toward the red brick buildings of Bay Street.

Flint leaned forward and called up to the little man. "Which of my women is it?"

"It's Elaine MacBride—the one who claimed that she was Scottish royalty."

"But that was eight years ago." Flint remembered back to the woman. "Where is the boy?"

"The place where he was born and where I was keeping the woman for you."

"And where was that?"

"At the home of the midwife, Emily Smoot." The carriage clattered off the stones and then turned right onto the red brick roadway toward the first ward. "She told everyone that MacBride's little girl died with her mother at the birthing, but I uncovered the thing—that it was a boy and Emily has raised your spawn as her own."

"Why has it taken you eight years to discover this?"

"I arrested a man for starting a fight in a tavern. He didn't have the money to pay for the damage he caused, so his wife came to me begging for mercy."

"What did she offer you?"

"She told me about Joshua Smoot—your bastard son."

"That's his name—Joshua Smoot?"

"Yes."

"His name will be Thomas Flint."

Damon turned. "Pardon?"

"That's to be his new name—Thomas Flint." Flint leaned past Hobson to study the roadway ahead. "How much further?"

"Not much—another few minutes."

Hobson pulled the carriage to a halt under a massive live oak at the western outskirts of Savannah. "There" He pointed. "That's the midwife's home."

The house was small, measuring no more than three spans wide and five deep, with an extension at the rear. Its walls were wood frame that was covered with lapstrake siding, boat fashion.

Flint stepped to the tabby-paved street and barked a command at Hobson. "Come!" Flint turned and climbed the short stairs to the front door. He tried the latch, but the door was bolted fast. "Emily Smoot!" He banged on the door with the butt of his flintlock. "Open this door!"

There was a pause, and then the faint and fearful voice of a woman answered. "Who is it?"

"I'm John Flint! You have my son!" He tried the latch again. The peg was set firmly in the slide. "Open this door, or by the gods, I'll break it in!"

"Please leave us alone!" She glanced to where Joshua and Sarah were reading and practicing their sums.

"I warned you!" With a single kick, the door flew back on its hinges, knocking Emily back against the Hickory table and then down against the wall. Flint thundered inside and looked about while Sarah—the older of the two children—ran to her mother.

"Your head! You're bleeding, mother!" Sarah held up a bloody hand to the pirate. "Look what you've done!"

"I gave her a chance to open the door."

"What do you want from us?"

While Hobson held Joshua in an armlock, Flint grabbed a chair and threw it aside. He stepped to the wounded woman, gave her a vicious kick to the leg, and pointed across at Joshua. "I want what belongs to me—my son, Thomas Flint!"

"Joshua is my son! I gave birth to him!" She pointed to the shelf with the journals. "Look for yourself—the journal with 1748 on the spine. It tells about your little girl—how she was stillborn and her mother died later that same day!"

"That's a lie!" Hobson pulled the journal from the shelf and brought it to Flint. "One of your neighbors swore on her Bible that Elaine MacBride was the only pregnant woman in this house!"

"Aha!" Flint looked to the little man. "Give it to me!"

"Her lie is on the first page." He handed the journal to Flint, and then pulled Joshua back beyond Flint's reach. "There's the lie I told you about—that Elaine's baby was a girl and that she died."

"Ah, yes. The twenty-ninth of January 1748!" Flint read the entry. "Stillborn Girl." He tapped the page and continued reading. "Father: John Flint. Mother: Elaine MacBride. Mother died after giving birth from severe bleeding." He tore the page from the journal and held it in the face of the cowering woman. "This should have said that it was a boy—my son—and that he lived! You lied to me eight years ago, and if it was not for Constable Hobson—"

"She made me promise on the Bible to raise him as my own."

"Then you admit it!"

"Elaine didn't want her little boy to become a pirate!"

"Thomas is my son, and I'll be the master of his fate!"

"Please don't do this, John!" While she spoke, Joshua broke loose from Hobson, ran to Flint, and gave him a shove toward the door. "Go away, and never come back!"

"Well, well, Thomas. There's no doubt that my blood runs in your veins."

"My name is Joshua!" He looked at Emily and Sarah. "Why did you hurt my mother?"

"I hurt this woman because she lied to me, and nobody tells John Flint a lie and goes unpunished."

"Please!" Joshua gave the pirate another push. "Promise you won't hurt my mother again!"

"Very well." Flint chuckled. "I promise that I will never hurt your mother again." Flint turned to Hobson. "Take my son out to the carriage."

"Please!" Emily struggled to her feet. "I'm begging you."

"So…" He gave her a toothy smile. "I'll tell you what, Emily Smoot. For taking such good care of my boy all these years, I will grant you one promise also."

"The promise I want from you is that you not make him a pirate."

"You have my promise. Thomas Flint will be raised in England at Wakehurst Place by my good friend, Charles Lyddell. My son will receive a classic education and when he is a grown man, he will take his place among the upper class of society." Before she could say another word, he pulled his pistol and pointed it at her face. "According to Savannah's constable and your confession, you are not his mother." He pulled back the lock. "One question."

"What else could you possibly take from me?"

He looked at her belly. "Are you now with child?"

"No—and why should that concern you?"

"I admit that I am an evil man but not so evil that I would kill an unborn child for the treachery of its mother." There was a flash and an explosion. Emily Smoot was thrown backward against the wall where she slumped dead to the floor.

While Sarah screamed, Joshua tore himself from Hobson's arms and attacked Flint—biting him on the right hand. "You promised me! You promised that you would not hurt my mother!"

"I didn't hurt your mother." He pointed down at the bleeding corpse. "Your mother died the day you were born, and that woman pretended you were her son."

"You're the Devil!"

"I'm the Devil, you say?" Flint gave a laugh and a vicious backhand that sent Joshua sprawling to the floor at Hobson's feet. "I'm not the Devil. Satan is my little brother, and I taught him everything he knows!"

While Sarah continued to scream, Flint grabbed Joshua by the hair, threw him outside at Damon, and marched past to the carriage. He stopped and turned. Are you coming, or are you going to stand and gape at that dead woman all day?"

Hobson turned and pulled the boy toward the carriage. "Couldn't you have waited till I had the lad outside so he wouldn't see that?"

"Are you questioning me, Damon Hobson?"

"I..." Hobson knew he had already said too much.

"I meant for him to see me kill her! If he doesn't fear me, he'll never obey me!" With that, Flint climbed into the carriage and pulled the thirty silver coins from his pocket. "Here's your money, Damon."

The ride back to the docks took only minutes. Flint jumped down to the worn planking.

Ben stood at the dock checking the merchandise and receipts as the merchants left. "Did you find him—the boy you've been hoping for?"

"Aye." He pointed to the carriage. "That's Thomas Flint."

"Where did you find him?"

"Hobson found him living with the midwife who has been lying to me for these past eight years."

"If she was lying, then..?"

"Yes. I shot her in the face while the lad watched." He started up the gangway and stopped. "Bring the lad aboard."

Ben stepped across to the carriage and reached up for Joshua. "Come with me, Thomas."

"Wait!" The little man grabbed Joshua by the hair and turned him nose-to-nose. "Look at me, Thomas Flint! I am Damon Hobson—a man to be feared as much as your father! When you started growing in your mother's belly, Flint was done with her." He pointed west. "I kept your mother my prisoner, and when she wrote to her family for help, I took those letters!" The little man opened his fist and showed Joshua the coins. "You are John Flint's bastard, and I earned this money—all that you are worth—by delivering you to him!" He paused while he conjured his final words. "Look hard and remember me well Thomas Flint, because I did this to you!"

"Let him go, Damon!" Ben reached up and pulled Joshua away. "You earned your blood money! You have no reason or right to destroy the lad's soul!" Ben put a comforting arm around Joshua's shoulders and led him up the *Walrus* gangway to join Captain Flint. "Here's the lad, Cap'n."

"Our little excursion to Emily Smoot's home has changed everything, Ben." Flint looked about at the merchants as they carried away the crates and the prostitutes began plying their trade to the single crewmen. "Instead of laying by for a month here in Savannah, we will provision the *Walrus* and sail across the Atlantic to Brighton, England."

"What's at Brighton, Cap'n?"

"There's a man who owes me a great debt, and I'm going there to collect on it."

"What do we tell the married men? I know you didn't promise it, but they're expecting to have a full month with their families before we go back to sea."

"Those who choose to stay home can watch over the sale of the rest of our cargo."

"How long before we set sail?"

"At dusk, have John Silver move the *Walrus* down to my creek and offload the rest of the goods to my warehouse." Flint gave a slight nod. "I want to be under way as soon as we take on the necessary provisions for the crossing." He took Joshua by the arm, started toward his cabin but turned. "One other thing, Ben."

"Captain?"

"Bring me that chain—the one with the ring and the shackle."

"Aye, aye, Cap'n."

Once inside the master's cabin, Flint turned and spread his arms wide. "Well, Thomas, what do you think of your new home?" Joshua turned and surveyed the cabin. "Well?" There was a knock at the door. "Come!"

"It's me, Cap'n." He held a canvas bag. "Here's the chain you asked for."

"Bring it here and dump it in front of Thomas."

Joshua watched the chain spill from the bag. "What's that for?"

"I'm pleased you asked." Flint got up, walked to the lad, and picked up the two ends of the chain. "You have a decision to make."

"If it's my name, my decision is already made. Nothing you do to me will change my mind."

"Then this is how things will be. Thomas Flint will have free run of the *Walrus*. Joshua Smoot's ankle will be shackled to this chain. Thomas Flint will eat and drink the same food as me, but Joshua Smoot will eat bread and water. Thomas Flint will sleep here with his father in a soft bed while Joshua Smoot sleeps on the hard deck"

"You killed my mother." Joshua held up a foot. "I will take your chain before I take your name."

"Then you have chosen to be my prisoner rather than my son." Flint attached the shackle to Joshua's ankle, tightened the screw, and held up the key. "So be it." Flint took the ring at the other end of the chain and attached it to a hook in the overhead. He eyed the lad for a moment and then pointed at a spot near the door. "Until we get underway for England, you will sleep there, and you'll do your animal functions in the same pot you eat from."

CHAPTER TWO:
The Crossing

The *Walrus* remained at Jacobson's dock for the rest of that day, and then once the merchant's money ran out, the pirate ship was ferried down the shore of the Savannah River for nearly a mile to the inlet of Flint's Creek. Two large warehouses and a counting room stood just to the west of the creek and accepted the rest of the booty taken at sea.

For strategic purposes, Flint's Creek was the perfect place to store both his ship and the vast store of wares that the town could not yet afford. Since Flint owned the creek, the Roman pump, and the four dikes and gates that controlled its flow, he enjoyed a lucrative tribute from the several rice plantations when they needed their fields periodically flooded and drained during the growing season.

A small crew was put aboard each of the Spanish prize ships, and just after breakfast three days later, the ships set their sails and began their separate journeys—the two Spanish ships north to the Carolinas where they would be sold, and the *Walrus* headed for Brighton on the south coast of England.

John Flint stood on his quarterdeck watching Little Tybee and Wassaw Islands fade in the morning sun. Ben stepped to his side and stood silent for several minutes. The thin man had learned long ago that it was best to allow his captain to bring up the subjects of conversation.

"I'm nearly thirty-six years old, Ben."

"Aye." Ben scratched his head. "That would make me nearly thirty-five." Ben hoped he would seem intelligent with his quick grasp of his sums.

"I've met hundreds of people in my life—the weak and the strong, the meek and the stubborn."

"You talkin' 'bout me, Cap'n?"

John turned and looked at his first mate for a moment and then back to the islands of Georgia. He shook his head. "I've run up against cleaver schemers like John Silver, and against addled women who act as dumb as hens or cows."

Ben began to say something stupid but held his tongue and flinched involuntarily at the thought of his captain's back-hand. "Aye—hens and cows." He nodded and gave the older man a worried smile.

"I didn't think I'd ever admit to something like this, but that damned boy—the one who's chained in my cabin below—is by far the most stubborn I've ever had fouled in my rigging." He shook his head in disbelief. "He doesn't cry. He doesn't beg for mercy, even when he's treated like a borrowed slave. Where the hell does that come from?"

"From you, Cap'n—from the blood that courses through his veins." Ben gave a twitch and an apologetic nod. 'Bein' yer spawn an' all, what else would ya be expectin' of 'im?" Ben scratched his scalp. "The lad comes by it naturally. Why, I'd wager a share of our next prize that he'll take to his rum ration the first time he tastes it, just like he took to his mum's teat, I do."

"I've never had anybody stand up to me like this."

"Can ya blame 'im, Cap'n?"

Flint stepped back from the rail and turned to Ben. "Hell yes I can blame him!"

"But what you done to his mum, right in front o' his eyes—" Ben knew he had said too much, but it was too late.

"That was meant to break his will!" Flint gave Gunn a dark look. "Are you suggesting I made a mistake?"

Ben swallowed hard. "I don't want to be telling ya what to do with yer own son, Cap'n but—"

"Then keep your scupper closed and let me think!" John turned his eyes back to the islands. "If seeing his mother killed hardened him, then there has to be some other way to break him."

Ben had waited for this moment. "There might be a way, Cap'n."

"Oh?"

"Since he hates you so much, what if I step between the two of you—kind'a like when Jesus stepped between the Devil an' a redeemed sinner?"

"Go on."

Ben felt good and relieved that his captain was willing to listen to one of his ideas. "If he refuses to repent from his old name to his new name, throw him out of yer cabin an' chain him to the mast. Then all ya have to do is wait."

Flint was interested. "Go on, Ben."

"Well, the way I see it, there's sure to be at least one charitable man aboard who'll sneak him food an' water. When you catch the man disobeying yer order, tell Thomas that it's his fault the man's to be flogged."

It took Flint a moment. "I'm not seeing it, Ben."

"The lad told me he learned to read usin' the Good Book. That means he knows about how Jesus suffered for other men's sin, an' that's sure to work on his soul." Flint just looked at his first mate. "Don't ya see it, Cap'n?" Ben turned around to demonstrate Joshua's change of direction. "He'll agree to change his name to save the man from the punishment he deserves."

"Are you suggesting I gamble the life of one of my crew on the chance Thomas will repent to prevent his flogging?"

"One of them will disobey your order, Cap'n, so you'll have to deal with it anyway."

"And what if Thomas still refuses to repent?"

"Well…" Ben had not thought that far ahead. "Then when ye're finished with the flogging, tell Thomas that he's next."

"You want me to flog my son?"

"No, Cap'n. That's when I step between you and the lad an' offer me own back in his place."

"So, you think that after Thomas will repent before he's made to watch you flogged?"

"He will if the two of us are close."

"How long will that take?"

"With me the only one allowed to bring him his food or speak with him, that should only be a few days."

Flint thought for a long moment. "It might work, but only if somebody sneaks him food and we catch him in the act."

"Oh, it'll happen, Cap'n. You can count on it."

"Before we do this, I want to try one more thing."

"Cap'n?"

"Thomas is starving. In the morning, bring me a double-sized breakfast with all the trimmings." He paused. "I like your plan, but the boy's stomach is working on his stubbornness."

☠ ☠ ☠

Ben arrived at the door of the main cabin at eight bells sharp with a tray of Captain Flint's breakfast—enough for both him and the eight-year-old. Ben tapped the door with the side of his foot. "You up, Cap'n? I got fried eggs an' sausage, boiled potatoes, toast, an' two kinds of preserves!"

"Come!"

While Ben walked across the cabin to the table, Joshua jumped to his feet at the rich smells. Ben set down the tray, pulled away the towels, and turned to the lad. "An' how's young Thomas this fine morning?"

Joshua stepped to the table and grabbed one of the boiled eggs. Just as his small fingers wrapped around the white orb, Flint grabbed his wrist. "Not so fast!" Joshua winced and gave a grunt of pain. "Before you eat a bite of my food, I want to know your name."

Joshua glared up at the evil man.

Ben gave a laugh and winked at the boy. "Why, everybody knows the pup's name! It's Thomas Flint!"

Joshua jutted his bottom jaw forward. "No, it isn't!"

Flint tightened his grip on Joshua's wrist until the egg dropped onto the tray. With a vicious backhand, Flint drove the boy backwards, away from the table. "It will be, or you'll starve to death long before we reach England!" John reached up and unhooked the end of Joshua's twenty-foot chain from the overhead and thrust it at Ben. "Take him! Fasten him to the mainmast, and make sure it's only bread and water until he begs to tell me his name!"

"Until...beggin' yer pardon, Cap'n, but how long are—"

"You heard me! I want his chain secured high on the mainmast. He'll stay there, and I don't give a damn whether the sun bakes him to a crisp or the rain and the cold soaks him to his bones!" He turned and gave the chain a jerk that threw Joshua forward in a sprawl. "Take him!"

"But..." Ben took the metal ring.

"Enough! You're a good mate, Ben Gunn, but the cat thirsts for your blood like any other man aboard the *Walrus*!"

Ben helped the boy to his feet and led him to the door. At the door, the pirate leaned down and whispered. "You sure you want this, Thomas? If you tell 'im yer name right now, this chain will come off and you'll share his food."

"Never!" Joshua reached down and grabbed up the twenty feet of chain, draped it heavily over his shoulders, and stepped into the passageway.

Ben looked back at Flint and shrugged. "I didn't think..." Flint slammed the door before Ben could finish.

To a man, every soul aboard the *Walrus* stopped trimming sails or tightening sheets as Otis, the smithy, reached up, set the ten-inch spike, and struck it with his great forging hammer. It was a hollow and mournful sound that reverberated throughout the ship—down the mainmast to the keel and then fore and aft through the deadwood and planking, back up through the bilges and ballast, finally playing itself out at the highest of the top gallants. It was a foreboding reminder of John Flint's meanness. The smithy took one last swing at the large spike and then looked down at the lad with all the pity he could muster.

"You!" Flint bellowed with a finger held out at the idle crew that stood and watched the spectacle. "Back to your duties! Those of you with no business topside, clear the main or taste the cat!" The smithy hesitated a moment too long at the mast. "And you!" Flint pointed at the large man. "Have you something to say?"

"No, Cap'n. The *Walrus* be yer ship, an' what's done aboard her is your word." He looked down at Joshua, and after a long moment knelt and whispered. "If you were my son, I'd—"

"Belay that!"

The smithy turned about to find Captain Flint nose to nose. "Captain, I didn't—"

"Break my rule concerning the lad and you'll earn the cat, Otis!" Flecks of saliva sprinkled the smithy's face. "Are the lad's circumstances worth that to you?"

"Honest, Captain Flint." The smithy backed away toward the larboard rail. "I had a son who died at about his age, and—"

"I'm not the Holy Spirit, Otis, so don't look to me for comfort!" Flint called out so the rest of the crew could hear. "The lad's name is Thomas Flint! Any man who feeds him or calls him by another name will taste the cat!"

Joshua sat inside the pin rail against the base of the great mast for an hour before John Flint finally came near enough to speak to him. "Get used to this, for until you declare to me that your name is Thomas Flint, you'll stand, sit, and sleep at this mast!"

Joshua continued to stare to lee at the passing water, as if Flint's words were only the passing wind.

"Nothing to say, have we?" Flint looked about the deck at the crew and then knelt beside the boy. "How dare you defy me in front of my crew?"

Joshua turned and looked up at the evil man. "My mother told me about the Boogey Man—that he would come and get me if I was bad. My sister told me that there was no Boogey Man, but now I do." He pointed. "You're him! You're the Boogey Man!"

"Ha! A few days ago, you called me the Devil." Flint leaned close. "Yes—I'm the Boogey Man your mother warned you about." Flint looked about at his men. "Ask any one of them! Ask them if you should fear me! Ask them what I do to people who do not obey me!" He looked at one man and then to another. "You! What do I do to those who disobey me?"

The man looked down at Joshua. "I saw him eat a woman's heart."

Flint turned back to Joshua. "The heat of the day, the cold of the night, and your own hunger will break you, Thomas! It's up to you how long you suffer before you crawl to me in repentance!"

Ben Gunn crept forward and knelt on the forward side of the mast, partially hidden from the captain. He leaned out just far enough to see if Flint was watching. He was. Ben gave an apologetic salute and looked away to weather.

Flint gazed upon his friend for several moments and then turned and marched aft, up the larboard ladder, and took his place on the quarterdeck. He called out above the passing sea. "You'll see, Ben Gunn! It'll take no more than a day and a night!"

The confrontation took only a minute at most, but those who ventured to watch the short battle of wills would later tell others far and wide, by ballad and story, that the two stood thus for a full glass before the lad finally turned his back on Flint and dragged his chain as far to windward as it would allow. And so continued the battle between the two stubborn souls—a battle that would last until John Flint's bones finally lay bleaching in the sun on the mud flats of the Savannah River.

"He's serious, Thomas." Ben leaned close and whispered. "Bread and water, and he'll leave ya chained to the main until we reach England if need be." Ben scratched a louse in his hair. "I'm no coward, mind ya, but there's a limit to what a man can take." He touched the boy. "You listenin' to Ben Gunn?"

Joshua turned, looked up at the quarterdeck. "If he had killed your mother like he did mine, would you take his name?"

Ben gave a nervous grunt. "I told him it was a mistake. I truly did."

"Answer me! Would you do it?" Joshua reached up and pulled at the chain. "Would you take his name to get rid of his chain?"

Ben looked at the small boy for an uncomfortable moment. "Where did you come from, lad?"

"From Savannah where I was free. Nobody has ever done anything like this to me."

"I'm askin' how such a big helping of stubbornness can live in such a little body?" Ben shook his head. "I've never met one like you—man or child. Even John Flint would change 'is name to whatever 'is keeper required to keep himself alive, warm, and with a full gullet."

"Answer me, Ben! Would you do it?"

"Aye." Ben nodded. "My soul cares more about life an' keepin' me belly full than a name."

"Are you proud of that?"

"Well, look at me!" Ben spread his arms and forced a smile. "I'm still alive, I'm clothed, and I seldom go long without a meal."

Flint's voice boomed down onto the main deck. "There'll be no whispering on the *Walrus*, Mister Gunn! It suggests sedition, and sedition always leads to mutiny!"

Ben jumped and bumped his head on the pin rail. "Oh, no, Cap'n! I was just telling young Thomas, here, how things were on board."

"Did you tell him how cold it gets in the northern latitudes? Did you tell him about the storms that will overrun us before we reach Brighton?"

"Aye, Cap'n! I told him all that!"

"Is he ready to step up here and tell me that his name is Thomas Flint?"

"I'm workin' on that, Cap'n!"

Joshua stood, walked aft toward John Flint as far as the chain would allow, turned, and called out to Ben. "I'm not like you or Ben! I'll not trade away my soul to get rid of this chain!"

"It's your name not your soul!" Captain Flint pointed a finger down at the boy. "Do you hate me that much?"

Joshua held up his chain. "This chain will never lie to me! This chain didn't kill my mother!" He shook the chain at the pirate. "Yes! I'll choose this chain and the fires of hell before I take your name!"

☠ ☠ ☠

As the days passed, Ben did the best he could to make Joshua's ordeal tolerable. As Flint had ordered, the lad was given a porcelain pot at the change of watch that contained his food and served for his nature calls. After two days at the mast, Ben was finally allowed to give the boy a mattress of fish nets.

It was not long before most of the ship's crew had found a reason to approach the mainmast and whisper a message to the boy. The messages were mixed, with most applauding Joshua's stand against Flint.

Jasper—the sailmaker—was the first to chance an encounter with Joshua. He was a man in his forties and one of the married men who chose to sail to Brighton on the promise that there would be additional prizes on the way back to Savannah. He stood two spans to leeward pretending to make a repair to the shrouds and rat lines. With a careful look about the deck to make certain nobody was watching, he whispered. "I know you're hungry. If I secret you some meat and fruit, will you protect me?"

"I'll eat anything!" Joshua rubbed his stomach. "Bring me a raw fish or a rat—anything with meat."

"You!" Ben walked across the deck to the man. "I heard the boy beggin' for food, Jasper."

"Ben's right, Thomas. You wouldn't want to see old Jasper trussed up an' whipped with the cat, would ya now?"

"He'd do that to you for a fish or a rat?"

"Aye." Jasper gave Ben a nod. "When Captain Flint gives an order, a man breaks it at his own peril."

"Get back to what you were doin', Jasper, an' leave the boy alone." Ben knelt next to Joshua. "The articles we signed when we joined Flint's crew be very strict on us, Thomas."

"Do they include starving a little boy just because he doesn't want to change his name?"

"Not in so many words, but we signed that we'd obey the captain until he be voted out, an' John Flint won't never be voted out 'till he be dead."

"I'm hungry, Ben."

"Cap'n Flint says it be bread and water for ya 'til ya repent."

"Why does he care so much about my name, Ben? Why is this so important to him?"

"If you were my son, I wouldn't care, but the man's just as stubborn as you, Thomas."

"He killed my mother and kidnapped me!" He picked up the chain and thrust it at Ben. "He put this chain on me!" He gave the empty plate a shove. "He's starving me, and as long as you do his bidding, you and the rest of the crew are no better than him."

"The truth be told?" Ben spoke softly, just above a whisper. "A man can't always do what he thinks is right."

"Why not?"

"You heard what the captain said—that any man caught talking to ya or sneakin' you food will be flogged."

"So, you're telling me that it's okay for a man to do what he knows is wrong, just to get along with somebody he's afraid of?"

"Men do what they have to do to keep living, Thomas."

"Kidnap, chain, and starve his own son?"

"Oh no, Thomas. This is a rescue, not a kidnapping."

"He killed my mother right in front me and my sister!"

"Aye, an act that was ill advised for certain. But that doesn't change the fact that—"

"Why do you act like a dog around him? Why do you lick his boots?"

"He's my captain, Thomas, and he's set me over you as yer caretaker."

"Stop calling me that name." Joshua turned away. "Leave me alone."

☠ ☠ ☠

It happened on the eighth night at just after eight bells. Joshua had become weak and was sound asleep on the bundled netting when a dark shape hovered over him.

"Joshua." It was a whisper and a nudge. "Wake up, Joshua."

The boy gave a groan and looked up at the man. "Ben?"

"Here." He held out a piece of folded cloth. "I brought you something."

Joshua looked up at the dark shape. "Who are you?"

"It's me, Jasper, the sailmaker." With a quick look to the quarterdeck to make sure he had not been seen by the watch, he ducked behind the mainmast and laid a small bundle on the deck under the pin rail. "Here. A few scraps of meat like you asked."

Joshua pulled at the knot and opened the cloth. There was an apple and a palm-sized piece of mutton. "Thank you, Jasper."

"It's not right how the captain's treating you."

"On deck at the mainmast!" It was the watch at the quarterdeck rail. "Who goes there?"

As Jasper slunk away forward, Joshua pushed the food under the net, and stood up. "It's just me, Joshua Smoot!"

"No! Who's that sneaking away forward?" As the watch called out, several others ran across the deck and intercepted the man.

"We got him!" They pulled him aft and called back. "It's Jasper Munson!"

"I was just up making a nature call."

"Check the lad!"

"Look here." One of the men held up the cloth and the food.

"What is it?"

"He brought the boy food." They pulled Munson to the ladder. "What do you want we should do with him?"

"Take him to the brig! Captain Flint's orders!"

☠ ☠ ☠

Joshua awoke at first light to the sound of a man begging for mercy. It was Jasper. He was standing with several others looking up at the quarterdeck.

"Please, Captain. Seeing the lad waste away like that was tearing out my heart."

"You knew the price for disobeying my order."

"It was just scraps, Captain, and the Good Book tells us to feed the hungry and them in prison, don't it?"

"The Good Book doesn't count when you sign articles with me."

"Have mercy on me, Captain."

"I'll give you justice, not mercy!" Flint called out. "I want all hands on deck to witness what happens to a man who disobeys my law." He turned to Ben Gunn. "Call me when everything is made ready."

It took less than ten minutes to assemble the crew and lash Jasper to a hatch cover set up at the rail. Ben called out as he led the captain forward. "Make a hole!" The crew pushed aside, opening a corridor from the captain's companionway to the mainmast.

Flint stopped next to Joshua and called out to the men. "Jasper Munson was caught last night secreting food to young Thomas." A murmur spread across the deck. "As you all knew on that morning that I had Thomas secured to the mast, I said that any man feeding him without my permission would be flogged!" He reached up and pulled the ring from the spike. "Come here, Thomas." He pulled the chain toward the assembled men. "I want you to see what this man's misdirected kindness has earned him."

Ben Gunn stood with two leather bags—one brown and the other black. "Here, Cap'n."

"You brought both cats?"

"Aye, so you could choose."

"No, Ben.' Flint stepped close and whispered. "This was your plan, so you will have to choose this time."

"Aye." He looked to Jasper for a long moment, turned back to Flint, and held out the black bag.

"Are you sure?"

"This is the only one that will do what has to be done."

"Then so be it." Flint handed the chain to Ben—trading it for the black leather bag.

Jasper twisted about. "How many, Captain? How many stripes does my charity to your son earn me?"

"How many?" Flint looked back at Joshua while he pulled the cat from the bag. Unlike the cat in the brown bag, this one had metal hooks woven into the ends of the nine braids. "Your disobedience has kindled a raging fire in me, so I'll flog you until that fire is quenched."

"Must the lad watch this?" Ben backed away slightly and gave Joshua a nudge to back away also. "Hasn't he suffered enough?"

"I'll know his suffering is enough when he agrees to change his name." Flint pointed to a spot on the deck. "Stand him here so he can see every blow."

Joshua bolted forward and stood between Flint and Jasper. "This should be my beating! Jasper only did what he did out of kindness to me!"

"Jasper disobeyed my order, so he will suffer for it!"

It took Flint a moment to untangle the braids. With a quick look around at the assembled crew to make certain everybody was watching—he stepped behind Jasper and raised his arm. "Behold! This is justice!"

With each stroke of the black cat, blood and pieces of the man's flesh fell onto the deck at Joshua's feet. After a dozen lashes, Jasper fell unconscious and hung limp against the hatch cover—portions of his spine and ribs laid bare to the elements.

Flint stopped whipping the dying man and turned to Joshua. "Is that enough, Thomas, or should I keep at it?" When there was no answer, Flint turned to the men standing to either side of the sailmaker. "Untie him!" Flint looked down at Joshua to make certain he was watching. "Let this be a warning to anybody else who is tempted to defy my orders about the lad!"

"He's dead, Captain. Jasper Munson is dead."

"Then throw him to the sharks."

While the crew began to disburse, Flint called out. "Belay!" The men stopped and turned. "There's one other matter you'll witness!" He grabbed Joshua by the hair and lifted him up and out through the open bulwark over the passing water to lee. Joshua reached up and grabbed Flint's wrist and forearm for support. "Tell me your name?"

"My name is Joshua Smoot!"

"Are you certain?" Flint gave the chain a kick out and into the passing water.

Joshua knew he was about to die, but for his mother's sake, he determined to take whatever came.

"This is your last chance, boy! If I let go, that chain will take you straight to hell with Jasper Munson!"

"No, John!"

"John?" Flint turned and scowled at Ben. "You haven't called me by my given name for years."

"You owe me a favor, John, and I want it now."

"Make it fast, Mister Gunn! I have a boy to kill!"

"Let me do it!"

"You want to kill him?" John looked at the lad and back to Ben. "This isn't your affair!"

"His name! Give him to me and he'll take his name before we reach England."

"And if you fail to do it, Ben, what will be the price you'll pay me for that failure?"

"You're the Cap'n! You name it!"

"Very well." Flint looked at the boy and back to Ben. "It'll cost you your heart!"

"You'd..?" Ben's shoulders slumped. "You'd eat my heart?"

"Well?" Flint gave the boy a rough shake. "Do I drop the whelp or do I give him to you?"

"The lad's worth my heart, Cap'n, but I want his chain off and for him to eat and bunk with me."

"Agreed!" Flint backed away from the rail, turned, and threw Joshua to Ben's waiting arms. "Here's the key to his shackle." While he turned away toward the ladder, Joshua fell to the deck while the chain pulled him mercilessly toward the ravenous sea, leaving Joshua's eight fingernail tracks in the worn teakwood. Nearing the edge and screaming for help, the crew let out a collective cry of unbelief at what John Flint had done.

CHAPTER THREE:
The Brighton Arrival

There was nothing Ben Gunn or the rest of the crew could do, but watch the horrible spectacle of Joshua being dragged by his ankle across the deck toward the sea and certain death. Joshua was being torn from the ship by not only the weight of the twenty feet of rusted iron links but by the current of the passing sea that pulled relentlessly at the chain. Several of the crew rushed forward, but Ben was the only one near enough to possibly make a difference. Ben scrambled across the planks toward the boy, but Joshua was just beyond his reach, sliding faster and faster as he neared the edge and the watery abyss that hungered for his little body.

The cries and gasps of a dozen crewmen were drowned out by the scream of Joshua's final plea for help. All that held Joshua from the sea were his fingernails tearing helplessly at the deck.

It was too late for heroics, and nobody saw it coming. In less than a second, Flint grabbed an eight-foot pike pole and threw it to the deck where it pierced Joshua's right hand and pinned him to the worn teakwood. With every crewman's eye on the evil man, Flint descended the ladder, walked across the deck, and stood over the boy. He looked around at the assembled crew and then bent down to the lad.

"You watched as I took Jasper's life for his disobedience. I shouldn't do this, but I am going to give you this one last chance." He took hold of the pike pole. "If Thomas Flint will repent and submit to take his name, he will be allowed to live without that chain, but Joshua Smoot's disobedience will take him to be with Jasper Munson." As one of the crewmen put his foot on the chain at the opening in the rail, Flint pulled his knife from its scabbard, leaned close, and pressed the razor-sharp blade to Joshua's wrist. "Choose, Thomas! Life or Le Tiburon!"

The eight-year-old looked at his hand. The pain of the pike through his flesh was almost more than he could bare, and he knew instinctively that it did not matter whether his hand was cut off or the pike was pulled free, because he knew the sea would take him either way.

"Well?" Flint drew his blade lightly across the tender skin to bring up a visible line of blood. "Life as Thomas or death as Joshua?"

Joshua turned his head and looked up at John Flint. He opened his mouth to answer, but before he could get this final refusal out, Ben grabbed onto the lad's free hand.

"We made a pact, Cap'n! You agreed that if I didn't get the lad to take his name before we reach Brighton, you'd eat my heart!"

Flint turned and looked at his first mate. His mouth bent upward at the right corner. "So, I did." Flint sheathed his knife, stood, and gave the crew a scan. "You hear that, Thomas? You take your name before we reach England, or I eat Ben Gunn's heart." With that said, Flint wrenched the pike from Joshua's hand, turned about, and strode away.

Joshua turned and yelled at his tormentor. "There will come a day, Captain Flint, that—"

Ben slapped a hand over the lad's mouth. "Hold yer tongue, Thomas!" He pulled the kerchief loose from his neck and wrapped it around the lad's wound. "If he's willing to cut off yer hand, he's willing to cut out yer tongue!"

"I mean it, Ben." Joshua leaned against Ben's chest and whispered through clenched teeth. "I'll see his bones scattered and bleached in the sun!"

"Keep that to yourself, Thomas." Ben took hold of the chain to pull it from the sea, but the man still held it with his foot. "Belay!" Once the foot was removed, Ben pulled it from the sea and back onto the deck. He turned and called. "Cap'n Flint!"

Flint stepped to the rail and looked down from the quarterdeck. "What?"

"His chain. You said it could come off."

"Are you accusing me of breaking my word in front of the crew?"

"No, Cap'n. I'd never do that."

"Very well." Flint plucked the key from his pocket and held it up. "Come up here and get it."

Aye, Cap'n." Ben climbed to his captain and reached out.

"I want Thomas to believe that I was trying to kill him, not that I threw the pike to save him from the sea."

"Then..?" Ben looked back at the boy. "Then you were truly aiming for his hand?"

"Yes, Ben. I want him to reach England alive, but fearing every day that I am willing to kill both him and you." Flint held up the key. "Can you do that?"

Aye, Cap'n."

"Here—take it and remove his chain."

"Thank you, Cap'n." Ben returned to the main deck, scooped up the boy, and whispered. "Do ya know how to pretend?"

"Pretend what?"

"I think I've figured the thing out."

"What thing?"

"It's a way to save my heart, your life, and you never have to tell the captain that your name is Thomas."

"Oh?"

Ben gave Joshua a grin. "Every time you an' me are around the captain, I will call you Thomas."

"And then what?"

"When I tell you to do something—to come or go, or to do a chore—I will call you Thomas."

"But you do that now."

"Aye, but from now on, when I give you one of those orders and I call you Thomas, you do the thing so Cap'n Flint thinks you've accepted your new name."

"I can do that but—"

"Don't ya see it?" Ben scratched his scalp. "The captain start thinking that you've accepted the name he put on ya, but this way, you'll never have to tell him so." He scratched under his arm. "After we leave you in England, you can do whatever you want about yer name." He touched his chest. "If we do this right, I'll keep my heart and you'll make it alive to Brighton."

Ben kept his hand over his heart as he looked down at the boy. "Someday, according to the Good Book, every one of us will kneel before the Lord and give an accounting, lad. You don't want my death added to your account, do ya?"

"I don't want you to die, Ben, but my name will always be Joshua Smoot."

"Then we're agreed?"

"Yes—we're agreed." Joshua looked at his injured hand. "Yes—I know how to pretend."

"Good!" Ben gathered up the chain and draped it over his shoulders. "You'll be livin' with me an' eating what I eat from now on 'till we reach England." He touched the boy's hand. "An' if I was you, I'd thank the Good Lord for the way he threw that pike."

"Why would I need to thank God for that?"

"He just told me that he was aiming for yer heart." Ben turned and called to one of the sailmakers. "You there, McAlister!"

"Aye?"

"Bring your kit to my cabin. The boy's hand needs stitchin' up."

By the time McAlister stepped into Ben's cabin with his kit, Joshua's chain was gone and his hand was soaking in rum. McAlister selected a needle and a span of thread and dipped them in the bowl of rum. "This will hurt but not as bad as that pike." He handed Joshua a folded leather belt. "Bite on this so you don't break any teeth."

"Uh…" Ben stepped to his cabin door. "I have some things to see to. Can you two manage without me?"

McAlister turned. "We'll be fine, Ben. Come back in an hour." The man pulled Joshua's hand from the rum and handed the goblet to him. "Here. Drink as much of this as you can. It'll help with the pain."

Joshua took a drink, gave a cough, and called to Ben. "I'm hungry, Ben. Can you bring me something better than moldy bread?"

Ben stopped in the passageway. He smiled at the lad's spunk. "Aye! He gave a wink. Maybe I can talk the cook into boiling you up the two fat bilge rats he was saving for me."

Joshua turned to McAlister. "What did my father mean when he asked if I was ready for *Le Tiburon*?"

"Le Tiburon is French for the shark."

☠ ☠ ☠

Ben walked aft to the master's cabin. He stopped, put an ear to the door, and listened. It was quiet. He had learned that if the captain was talking to stay away. He tapped twice.

"If that's you, Ben, come!"

"Aye." Ben pushed through the door and then closed it behind him.

"How's the whelp's hand?" Flint sat at the mess table with his fists clenched. The pike pole lay on the table between them. It still had Joshua's blood on it.

"It'll be alright, Cap'n. McAlister's stitching him up as we speak."

"Did he agree?" Flint ran his finger across the tip of the pike and then held up his bloody finger. "Is my plan working?"

"The pretending?"

"Yes, damn it!" He wiped the blood on the table. "Did he agree to go and come to his name?"

"Aye, Cap'n, an' I convinced him that you were aiming for his heart."

Flint pushed back the chair, picked up his tankard of rum, and walked to the window. "I should be proud of his determination—bastard and all—shouldn't I?"

"Aye, Cap'n." Ben gave a nod. "The crew respects your strong will, so you're right to be proud of the lad."

"He's…" Flint turned and looked squarely at Ben. "My Mum said I had the will of a dozen proud men." He returned Ben's nod. "Yes—I'm proud of Thomas for standing up to me." Flint could tell Ben was thinking of something deep. "What?"

"You wouldn't have dropped him into the sea today, would you?"

"No, but he and the crew must believe I would." Flint waited for Ben's answer. "There's something else bothering you, Ben. What is it?"

"The lad was willing to take Jasper's punishment, an' that's the kind of thing you'd do for me, Cap'n. A thing like that comes from only one place, an' that's from the blood that runs through his veins." Ben gave a knowing nod. "That's yer blood, Cap'n, an' any father would be proud of that."

"It does make me proud." He took a drink from his tankard. "Keep the lad close and play whatever games it takes to get him to take his name."

☠ ☠ ☠

On the 15th of June, after an uneventful crossing, the top watch sighted the Saint Agnes Isles of Scilly on the larboard bow. It would be two more days and the *Walrus* would arrive at Brighton, England. The wound in Joshua's right hand mended quickly but left a mean scar. For encouragement's sake, Ben had told Joshua what little he knew of the seaport and of his new home, but the boy only wanted to return to his sister in Savannah.

"I'm to be a slave, aren't I, Ben?"

"Have no fear, me boy. Ye'll be nobody's slave."

"But I heard him telling you about the money he already paid to the Englishman. When people sell people, that makes them property, and that makes them a slave."

"Ben put a comforting hand on Joshua's shoulder. "If he was gonna sell ya, the Lord o' Wakehurst would be givin' Cap'n Flint the bag o' gold, but there won't be any money passing hands for you."

Joshua thought for a long moment. "What will become of me, Ben?"

"Ah! As Thomas Flint, ye'll have all the finest things! Clothes of satin, shoes what were made by the best cobblers, and a feather from a peacock in yer hat! Ye'll eat lamb and pork with sweet yams from plates of fine China, and forks and spoons o' silver an' gold!" Ben took a long breath and let out a whistle. "By the blood of the holy martyrs, I'd trade ya places in a wink."

"Will I ever go home?"

"If yer talkin' about Savannah, I'd wager the next time you see the place is as a gentleman of means—a rich merchant or a banker."

"And if I refuse his name, will he kill you and eat your heart?"

"We made a blood covenant, and nobody breaks a blood covenant made with John Flint."

"If I go back to Savannah to see my sister, will you come to see me, Ben?"

"Aye!" Ben gave a reassuring chuckle. "That's Flint's and my home. It'll be you comin' to see us when you're grown and rich."

"He's an evil man." Joshua rubbed at the fresh scar on his right hand and held it up to Ben. "Look at my hand. Look at what he did to me."

"Any boy your age would be proud of a scar like that." Ben paused. "Think of the stories you can tell, and the envy those stories will spawn, 'specially it being the famous pirate, John Flint, what put it there."

"That's why I hate it so much, Ben." Joshua held up his hand and turned it about to look at both sides. "I'd just as soon he had cut my hand off that day and thrown it to the sharks."

"Careful what you wish for, me boy." Ben looked up, leaned close, and dropped his voice to a whisper. "It's a fact that the Good Lord don't listen much to low people like what you came from—an' I'd wager He listens less to pirates like me for where I am right now." He gave Joshua a wink and a flick to the nose. "But then—He could be *listenin'* to us right now, so we'd best be watchin' what we wish for."

☠ ☠ ☠

The crossing from Savannah to Brighton took seven arduous weeks. While the *Walrus* stood off Brighton by two leagues, John Flint met with two of his men to finalize their mission.

"You'll take this map with you." Flint put the tip of his knife on the port of Brighton and traced a line north. "Ardingly is sixteen miles north of Brighton, and Wakehurst Place is on the north edge of the town." He looked up at the two. "We will take the *Walrus* near the east docks where you two will board the skiff. When you reach the docks, you will take the money I have given you and buy a horse and carriage. Once you reach Lyddell's mansion, you will wait until you are certain everybody has retired to bed."

"What if Lyddell or his staff fights us?"

"That is why I chose you and Taylor." He looked at the other man. "You both have the reputation for sneaking into buildings to plunder them at night without being caught. Lyddell should be asleep, so it should not be too difficult to take him captive." Flint tapped the map. "When you get back to the dock with him, I want you to begin signaling us with your two lanterns."

It took Cooper and Taylor an hour to find Wakehurst Place. As instructed, they waited until the last window went dark, left their carriage a hundred yards away, and entered the mansion through the kitchen. After opening two of the rooms and finding them vacant, they heard snoring.

"This is his room." Cooper drew his knife, eased the door open, and crept to the bed.

Charles Lyddell jerked awake at the cold steel pressed against his neck. "What the—?"

"Shush or die!" Cooper pressed the dull side of his blade against the older man's throat. "Have you decided which it will be, Lord Lyddell?" Charles mumbled his agreement and nodded his head. "Good." Cooper pulled away his hand and stood back. "Dress quickly because we are going on a carriage ride."

"What is this? Who are you? Where are you taking me?"

"Your questions will be answered soon enough. For now, you need to get dressed or go in your night gown."

Ten minutes later, the two led Lyddell down through the kitchen, across the courtyard, and out to their carriage. An hour later, the three arrived back at the docks. As instructed, Cooper and Taylor gave the lantern signal to the *Walrus*.

"Did they see it?"

"I just did it, Taylor. Give them a chance to respond." As they watched, the signal was returned. "There! They'll be on their way in a few minutes."

"Hey, you two!"

"What?" Cooper set the lanterns down and walked back to the carriage. "If you're gonna ask us again who we brought you here to meet, I'm going to have to get mean." He gave a smile and a shake of his head. "You don't want to see me when I'm mean."

"Can you at least untie me?"

"Only if I have your word that you won't try to run away."

"And just where would I run?"

"Make your promise or you stay in those bindings until they get here."

"Alright! I promise!"

It took several minutes to untie the knots and for Lyddell to get his circulation going to his hands and feet. As he stepped down onto the dock, the three could hear the oarlocks on the boat as it drew near.

Lyddell stepped to the edge of the dock and peered out into the darkness. "Hello!" There was no answer. "I know you're coming to see me, but your two men would not tell me who you are!" There was still no answer. He turned back to Cooper and Taylor. "I don't care if you get mean, Cooper." He pointed seaward. "Who is that in the boat?"

"Ahoy! On the dock!"

Lyddell spun around and looked at the approaching boat. "This is Charles Lyddell! Your two men kidnapped me and brought me here against my will! Who are you, and what do you want from me?"

The boat bumped against the ladder. There was a moment of shuffling and then a head appeared at the top of the ladder. "Good evening, Charlie. Remember me?"

"John Flint?"

"Aye." Flint pulled himself up onto the dock and spread his arms. "In the flesh."

"You did this to me?" He pointed at Cooper and Taylor. "You sent these two apes to kidnap me and—"

"Careful, Charlie! From everything I see, they did exactly what I told them to do."

"Your men broke into my home—into my bedroom for God's sake. Then they forced me to get dressed, sneak through my own home like a thief, out to their carriage, and here to the dock!"

"Did either of them hurt you?" Flint searched the man for injuries. "I don't see any bruises."

"Yes—my dignity!" He looked at the others as they gained the dock. "Who are these two?"

"This is my first mate, Ben Gunn."

"And the lad?"

"This is my son, Thomas Flint, the object of this affair."

"I don't understand. What does your son have to do with me?"

"It's the blood covenant you made with me the day I saved you and this estate from your creditors."

"That was years ago."

"But when a man makes a promise to me, I never forget." He pulled a folded parchment from his waistcoat pocket. "Allow me to refresh your memory, Charlie." He picked up one of the lanterns and held it up as he read.

I, Charles Lyddell, Lord of Wakehurst Place, hereby make this blood covenant with John Flint, that in exchange for paying my gambling debt and saving me from my creditors, I will repay his kindness by doing whatever he asks of me—short of murder—without objection or reservation. Charles Lyddell.

"Yes, I remember that." He looked at Joshua and back to the pirate. "What do you require of me?"

"I have never been married, but I have spawned a half dozen or more children with various women. All were born girls, except for this lad."

"Go on."

"As much as I enjoy my life as a pirate, I want Thomas to have a better life than me."

"And how does that involve me?"

"To repay your debt to me, I require that you to take him in and raise him as if he is your own son."

"You want me to adopt him and give him the Lyddell name?"

"No. He is to keep his name—Thomas Flint."

"Never!" Joshua pulled away from Ben's grip and backed away from the five men. "I will never take that name!"

"A spirited lad." Charles gave a laugh. "I believe he's better suited to follow you back to sea and piracy than to follow me and my ways."

"You made a blood covenant, Charles." Flint paused. "Do you know what that means?"

"I believe so but remind me."

"It means that if you refuse, then you pay with your life's blood."

"So, if I do this thing for you—raise your bastard son to be like me—my debt to you is paid in full?"

"It's not an *if* thing, because you have no choice in the matter." He pointed at Joshua. "Furthermore, you will never call him a bastard after this moment. Thomas is my son whether I was married to his mother or not."

"So, that's it? My obligation is to give him a classic education, that I teach him how to fit into high society, and to grow up to be a gentleman like me?"

"Yes—just like you." Flint pushed Joshua forward to the Englishman.

"Well, then." Charles looked down at the boy. "Thomas Flint, your life is about to change for the better."

"Didn't you hear me?" Joshua looked at Flint and back to Lyddell. "My name is Joshua Smoot!"

Charles looked at Flint. "Uh, is that going to be a problem?"

"Not once he repents and accepts his name."

"And if he doesn't?"

"You have my permission to punish him however you wish—short of killing him."

"Like what?"

"Take a switch to him every time he calls himself Joshua Smoot."

"And if he still refuses to be called Thomas Flint?"

"Then put him to hard labor until he repents."

"And if he still refuses?" Charles gave John a slight grin. "I could sell him for several hundred pounds and we could split the take."

"No! You may punish him for his disobedience as you see fit, but only I have the right to sell him or take his life." Flint reached across and took Charles' throat in his hand. "If Thomas dies in your custody, you will die in mine."

Charles wrenched the hand free and stumbled away. "As you say, Captain Flint. As you say." He looked down at Joshua. "Since I'm driving, Thomas, you can ride in the back or up front with me."

"I'll…" Joshua looked across at the carriage. "Up front with you."

Charles turned to Flint. "Are we finished here?"

"Yes, and you can both be assured that I will return someday without warning to check on his progress."

Joshua kicked Flint in the shin, turned, and ran to the carriage.

A moment later, Charles Lyddell cracked the whip and drove the carriage away from the Brighton dock. Once past the edge of town, he turned to Joshua. "Can we reach an agreement—an agreement your father never has to know about?"

"What kind of agreement?"

"Neither of us asked for this, but since we are deep inside it, we have to make compromises."

"What does that word mean—compromises?"

"It means we each have to do what we don't want to do in order to keep the other one safe and happy." He slowed the carriage to cross a stone bridge. "Your father has forced me to take you and raise you as if you are my son. I do not want to do that, but I will because I do not want your father returning to kill me. Likewise, you have been forced into my custody against your will, and I know that you do not want it any more than me. Your compromise is to cooperate and take the name Thomas Flint. If you refuse, I will punish you when and how I please until you repent."

"Did he tell you what he did the day he took me from Savannah?"

"No." He pointed back toward Brighton. "You were there and heard everything that was said."

"My older sister and I were reading when John Flint began yelling at the front door. Then, when my mother refused to open it to him, he kicked it open and hurt her head. She was bleeding, and after more yelling about me, he made Sarah and me watch him shoot her in the face."

"Oh, my Lord!"

The two rode on without a word.

CHAPTER FOUR:
Lord Lyddell's Wakehurst Place

*I*n the year 1205, William Wakehurst was bequeathed four-hundred acres of land in Ardingly, West Sussex, England where he built the thirty-two-room mansion which bears the family name to this day. For the next five centuries, Wakehurst Place was owned and occupied by a variety of families—first the descendants of William, and then through the lack of male heirs, the estate was bequeathed to the Culpeper family in 1510, and finally on 6 June 1694 it passed to Dennis Lyddell and his family for L9,000.

By the time Dennis acquired Wakehurst Place, its lands had increased to eleven hundred acres, to which he added at least another two thousand, as well as buying back the Naylands estate in Balcombe and other land there. He and his wife, Martha, had five children—two girls, Elizabeth and Frances who died in infancy, and three sons, Richard, Charles, and William. Dennis died in 1717 and two years later, upon Martha's death, all his property went to his eldest son, Richard.

Richard was a rascal, mortgaging Wakehurst Place and borrowing heavily from his sister Elizabeth, and his brother Charles. Unable to repay his debts, Richard's ownership of Wakehurst fell to the bachelor, Charles in 1731. Finding the estate deep in debt, Charles sold several hundred acres along the eastern borders and arranged a visit with his cousin, Richard Blake, at Portsmouth in 1742 to secure a personal loan. By coincidence, the pirate ship *Walrus* was in port selling a Spanish prize ship and its cargo to the local merchants. Richard never missed one of these sales and insisted Charles accompany him to the docks. While Richard was arguing with Ben Gunn over the price of several bolts of silk brocade, Charles met the young pirate John Flint, and struck up a friendship. That friendship led to a blood covenant between the two.

☠ ☠ ☠

The carriage thundered along the road that led north out of Brighton. After twenty minutes of silence, Charles gave Joshua a nudge. Joshua looked up at him.

"What did your mother do to John Flint to make him shoot her?"

"I don't know what she did wrong to deserve it, but after he kicked down the door and hurt her head, he shot her in the face with his pistol."

"And he made you watch him do it, right?"

"Yes—I told you that!" Joshua nodded. "The man who came with him read something about me in a book, and that's when Flint killed my mother, even though he promised me that he would never hurt her again."

"Did your father tell you anything about England and your new home?"

"No, but Ben Gunn told me that I would have the finest of everything a boy could want."

"Ben was right. I am obligated to your father to educate and raise you as a gentleman."

"How do you do that?"

"Well, I would imagine the first thing after we clean you up, will be to teach you to sit at a dining table and eat without embarrassing me or the lords and ladies of privilege. Then your formal studies will begin."

"What kind of studies?"

"Do you know how to read and write?"

"Yes." Joshua nodded. "My mother taught me to read the Bible, write out verses, and to do my sums."

"Good!" Charles thought for a moment. "There's so much more. You'll learn the steps to a dozen different dances, and there'll never be a tune played that you won't already know. You'll learn to ride a horse over hill and dell, as they say, to shoot pheasants and foxes, and to catch trout in your own lake."

"What about the studies?"

"Oh, everything! You'll learn astronomy, the history of England and the world, the earth sciences, philosophy and how governments operate, mathematics, accounting, and how to speak and read Latin." Charles spread his arms wide. "In short, under my guidance, you will experience a transformation very few lads your age have been privileged to receive." He took a large breath and let it out slowly. "When your father finally comes back for you, you will be a gentleman in every sense of the word."

"Will I have my own horse?"

"Of course, you will. And you'll be able to name and recognize all the various breeds."

"Will I have my own room with my own clothes and toys?"

"There are over a dozen empty bedrooms in Wakehurst Place. Except for my rooms, you can have your pick."

"There's one other thing."

"Oh, I'm sure you'll have a thousand and one other things to ask of me."

"I have one question I need answered now."

"So serious!" Charles gave the boy a narrow look. "Ask!"

"Will you allow me my real name, or will you do as my father has done to me?"

Ha!" Charles gave a dismissive laugh. "What's in a name?"

"If your father killed your mother in front of you, and demanded that you take his name, would you obey him?"

"That depends on several factors, but off hand my first reaction would be the same as yours."

"Then you agree with me that I should keep my name."

"But then again, I'm a practical man, so it would ultimately depend upon how my decision affected my well-being." Charles studied the boy. "I can see that you don't like my answer."

"No." Joshua shook his head. "You are not me."

"Well, never you mind." Charles gave a grin and rubbed Joshua's hair. "After you get cleaned up, into your new clothes, have chosen your bedroom, and are immersed in your training and studies, you'll see differently, won't you?"

"Never!"

"Listen to me, Thomas, and I'll say it just once. We both heard your father's instructions regarding your name and what I'm to do if you defy me. Now, you can cooperate and have a wonderful life at Wakehurst Place, or you can make this the most miserable time of your life. Choose well, Thomas Flint. Choose well."

☠ ☠ ☠

It was still dark when Charles turned the carriage into the driveway from the southeast and circled past the corrals and stables. He was met at the front door portico by the butler, the footmen, and all the house servants, still dressed in their bedclothes and robes.

The stable master—John Manley—grabbed the horse's reigns and called up to his master. "Where have you been, sir, and where did you get this carriage?"

"To the Brighton docks and back." He dropped the reigns. "This is now my carriage."

The butler stepped close and looked to Joshua. "Who is the lad?"

"His name is Thomas Flint. Two men…" He shook his head. "I'm tired, I'm angry, and I choose not to explain myself or the boy to any of you until I am rested." He turned to the footman. "Take the boy inside, turn him over to the maids, and see that he's bathed, properly dressed, and ready to join me at breakfast."

"Yes, sir." The footman reached up and pulled Joshua down to the ground. "Come with me, Thomas."

Charles followed Joshua and the footman to the porch where the butler pulled open the massive door. "Sir?"

"Yes, Graves?"

"The butler looked down at Joshua. "May I ask where you found the lad, and why you've brought him here to Wakehurst Place?"

Charles stepped close and lowered his voice. "I didn't *find* him. He was brought to me."

"What does that mean, sir?" Graves and the other servants traded questioning looks. "The lad was brought to you?"

"Come!" Charles stepped into the study, turned, and waited.

"Are you in some sort of trouble, sir?"

"Only if I fail at the task that was forced upon me."

"Forced? What does that mean?"

"Do you remember John Flint—the pirate who paid the debt I owed to prevent the loss of Wakehurst Place to my creditors?"

"Of course, I do."

"Thomas is John Flint's bastard, and to get my debt satisfied, I signed a blood covenant with the pirate promising that I would pay back my debt to him whenever and however he required."

"A blood covenant? Like in the Old Testament?"

"Yes, and if I do not fulfill my promise, I will forfeit my life." Charles paused. "Two of Flint's men came to me around midnight, forced me from my bed, and drove me down to the Brighton docks in their carriage." He pointed toward the foyer. "My obligation to John Flint is that I raise Thomas as if he is my own son."

Graves gave a disapproving grunt.

"What?"

"Since you are whispering this to me, I must assume that you want your kidnapping kept from the staff."

"I'm certain they will learn of it eventually but not now."

"Very well, sir."

"I am going to lie down for a few hours." Charles looked at the clock. "Wake me at eight, and have Thomas washed up, dressed, and brought down to share breakfast with me."

"As you wish, sir."

"One other thing, Graves."

"Sir?"

"The boy has grown up using the name Joshua Smoot. My agreement with John Flint is that he takes the name Thomas Flint. You will therefore inform the staff that as long as the lad shares my home, anyone who calls him by that other name shall be sacked and sent away without a reference."

"I understand, sir."

One of the maids stepped to Joshua. "Good morning, Thomas. My name is Jersey." Joshua would not answer. "You're a cute lad, but you smell like a wet dog who has been playing with the chickens and pigs." She waited. "Cat got your tongue, Thomas?" He glared at her. "Well then, we've quite a job to get you ready for breakfast with Lord Lyddell, don't we?"

By nine o'clock, Jersey and the other maids had trimmed Joshua's hair, given him a long-overdue bath, and dressed him in the clothes of a child who had died of the influenza a decade before. Jersey took Joshua to the dining room and stood him behind one of the chairs.

"I know I already told you all this during your bath, but to make certain you don't embarrass yourself and get me into trouble with Lord Lyddell, I will show you what I meant."

She touched the chair. "You will wait to be seated until Lord Lyddell takes his seat." She pulled out the chair, motioned for him to sit, and sat in the chair next to him. After you sit down, you will follow the master's lead. When he takes his napkin, you will take yours, unfold it, and spread it across your lap." She demonstrated how it was to be done. "Do everything slowly, because when you do things too quickly, you will make mistakes, and I will be held responsible for those mistakes." She gave him a squint. "You don't want me to be in trouble, do you, Thomas?"

He just looked at her.

"You have to understand what this is, Thomas. Lord Lyddell has agreed to certain things with your father—things that could cost him dearly." She waited. "You may not like any of this, but like it or not, this is your new life."

Graves stepped to the door and gave Jersey a nod. "He's coming!"

Jersey stood, pulled Joshua to his feet, and pushed in the two chairs. "I'm going to leave you to the footmen, but I will be listening from the pantry. Please don't embarrass me."

"Ah!" Charles strode into the room and stopped behind his chair. "Can that be the same boy who rode beside me from Brighton?"

"It's Thomas Flint, bathed, trimmed, and dressed as you required, sir."

"And is he hungry enough to share breakfast with me?"

Jersey nodded. "He won't say so, sir, but his stomach is telling me that he's more than ready."

"Well, then!" Lord Lyddell took his seat and signaled for the footmen to serve the food. "Shall we eat?"

The two footmen set several covered serving platters on the sideboard and removed the lids. The room was suddenly filled with the smell of fried bacon and freshly baked rolls.

"Wait!" Charles held up his hand to the footman with the plate of fried eggs. "There's one matter we must address before we partake." Joshua clasped his hands in front of him and closed his eyes in anticipation of the prayer. "No— we'll get to the blessing in a moment." He leaned forward. "First, tell me your name."

Joshua looked to Graves first. The man was like carved ice. He looked to Jersey next. She gave him a dark look. He looked at the food and finally into the eyes of his new master. He took a large breath and said the words slowly. "My name is Joshua Smoot."

"Graves!" Charles leaped to his feet and pointed at the boy. "Remove this disobedient child from my table, take him to the kitchen, and beat him with a switch until he repents!"

"What about his food, sir?"

"A little boy named Thomas Flint is welcomed to everything on my table, but a gutter snipe named Joshua Smoot is not!" Charles glared at the butler. "The whipping will be the only breakfast he receives!"

"Very well, sir." Graves grabbed Joshua by the arm and pulled him from his chair.

Charles tucked his napkin in his collar. "Perhaps the blueness of your wounds will soften your will so that you can join me for dinner this evening!" Charles filled his plate with food and took a bite. "If not, I have other means at my disposal to break your will."

CHAPTER FIVE:
A Dung Boy's Beating

Graves brought Joshua back to the dining room after his beating and stood him behind his chair. As ordered, both footmen and the upstairs maids were present.

Lord Lyddell stood at the window looking out onto the drive and the front gates. He spoke without looking around at the lad. "Have you learned anything from your beating?"

Joshua stood silent.

"I suppose if I was as hungry as you must be, I'd have difficulty speaking also." Charles turned, walked to the head chair, and sat down. He nodded to the butler for the serving plates to be uncovered once again. "Unfortunately, you are not only hungry, but now your back stings of the switch." Joshua would not answer but surveyed the food before him.

"I am a forgiving man, Thomas." Charles picked up a link of sausage and took a bite. "Mm!" He looked at Graves. "Delicious!" He turned to Joshua. "If my calculations are correct, you haven't eaten for over thirty hours."

Joshua's stomach gave a vicious growl. There were fried eggs, biscuits fresh from the oven, a boat of white gravy, sausage links, bacon strips, freshly churned butter, three flavors of preserves, a plate of fresh fruit, and finally a pitcher of warm milk. The aromas were overwhelming.

"Like I told you before your whipping, I am a gracious man. As our Savior instructed his disciples to forgive, so do I." He sat back, wiped his mouth with his napkin, and opened his Bible. "The Jews had a problem with forgiveness of one another, so Jesus told them this." He looked down and read. "If thy brother trespass against thee, rebuke him; and if he repents, forgive him." He looked up but kept a finger on the page. "Your trespass is refusing to take the name your father has decreed. I have rebuked you for that." He tapped the page. "Now, it is time for you to repent of that refusal. When you do that—tell me that your name is Thomas Flint—I will forgive you, treat you like my son, and we will eat this delicious breakfast."

Charles waited while Joshua wiped the last tears from his cheeks.

"What happened a few minutes ago in the kitchen is in the past. We are starting fresh."

With a quick glance to see where Graves was standing, Joshua reached out his scarred right hand, grabbed a fist full of bacon, and brought it to his mouth.

"Not so fast, young man!" Graves grabbed Joshua's forearm and turned to Charles. "Sir?"

Charles spread butter on a hot roll and took a bite. "Shall I take that—your handful of bacon—as your repentance?"

Joshua knew what was coming next. He tried to twist loose from Graves' grip, but the man's hand was like a carpenter's vise. "I'm hungry."

"Of course, you're hungry, but *I'm hungry* is not your name, so try again, and then you can eat anything you please."

Joshua looked down at his arm and back to Charles. "I'll give you your answer when he lets go of me."

Charles considered and then nodded to Graves.

Graves gave the lad's wrist a squeeze. "You'll drop the bacon first!"

Joshua opened his fingers and then pulled his arm back. Graves' hand print had depressed Joshua's skin, leaving it white and hollow. Joshua rubbed at the pain.

"Well?" Charles took another bite of the roll. "Do you tell me your name, or do you go hungry again?"

Joshua stared at Charles for a full minute and then pulled the napkin from his neck. Without a word, he slid to the floor and walked to the pantry door where Jersey had been standing throughout the entire drama. Joshua stopped, turned back to his new master, and held up his scarred right hand. "John Flint killed my mother while I watched, and he pinned this hand to the deck of the *Walrus* with a pike. I won't let him take away my name too, and I don't care what you do to me."

"Are you so certain of that?" Charles wiped his mouth with his napkin and stood.

"Yes—I am certain!"

"Very well!" Charles turned to Graves. "Are his dirty clothes still about?"

"We threw them out with the trash, sir." He looked at the footman. "I told Alexander to burn them."

Charles turned and looked to the young footman. "Did you?"

"No, sir, not yet. I don't burn the trash until after breakfast."

"Good!" Charles stood pointed at the boy. "Take those clothes off and dress him in those old things he came in."

Graves looked to the footman and back to Charles. "But he'll stink, sir. We can't have him in the house smelling like the garbage."

"He won't be in the house."

"Oh?"

As the footman took Joshua away, Charles pointed toward the stables. "Bring me John Manley."

"As you wish, sir."

Moments later, the stable master stood next to the butler's pantry as ordered. Lord Lyddell set down his fork and looked to the elderly man. "Manley! Thomas has disobeyed my orders. Shortly, Graves will bring the lad to the stables. You will work him sixteen hours every day and beat him like you did that orphan very time he tells you his name is Joshua Smoot." He pointed. "Go!"

"As you please, sir."

Graves took Joshua by the ear and jerked him to the stairs. At the boy's room, Graves began to unbutton Joshua's new blue velvet waist coat. "You don't know what your stubbornness has cost you, Thomas, and with that temper and contentious spirit of yours, I doubt you ever will." In a moment, Joshua stood naked in the middle of the room. Alexander entered the room and handed Graves the bundle of clothes.

"Here!" Graves threw the garbage-stained clothes at Joshua's face. "Do you like the smell of your stubbornness? Do you prefer the memories those stinking rags bring back rather than the privileged life Lord Lyddell has offered you?"

Joshua stood naked for a long moment before he slipped into his rough trousers.

"The stable keeper will have you mucking the stalls of dung! A fitting labor for your kind, I suppose!"

The moment Joshua finished tying the rope at his waist, Graves grabbed him by the same ear and marched him down the back stairs, through the kitchen, and out the servant's entrance to the courtyard. Graves spotted Ned filling his water buckets at the cistern.

"You—Ned! Take Thomas to the stables and tell Manley to put him to work!" With that, Graves pushed Joshua to the ground and gave him a rough kick to the hip. "I give you a week and you will be begging me to take you back to Lord Lyddell!"

"Never!" Joshua leaped up, doubled up his fist, and attacked the butler.

A hard backhand sent the boy sprawling to the cobblestones. Before he could push himself up, Graves stepped on his neck. "If it weren't for my master's blood covenant with your father, I should kill you right now, you ungrateful little bastard!"

Just then, John Manley walked from the stable doors. He stopped and looked down at Joshua. "Whatever the boy's done, it doesn't give you license to push him down into the mud like a dog." Graves was a small man. He stepped away from the older and larger man. "How long do I have him?"

"As long as it takes!"

"As long as what takes?"

"As long as it takes him to accept his new name—Thomas Flint."

"That's all this is about—the lad accepting his father's name?"

"The master wants him doing the lowest, the dirtiest, the most disgusting chores you have for him!" Graves turned and started walking across the cobblestones but stopped. "He'll repent of this stubbornness, or else." Graves turned and began again toward the servant's entrance.

John called after him. "Or else what?"

Graves stopped and pointed up. "As Thomas Flint, the lad will live the life of luxury, attend the finest schools, and enter society as a gentleman." He pointed across at the stables. "As Joshua Smoot, he will muck dung in the stables like the worthless bastard he is!" Graves took several steps back toward Manley. "If young Thomas fails to repent and ever says his old name to me or Lord Lyddell again, you will be held responsible."

"Are you saying I could be punished for the lad's conduct?"

"That is what Lord Lyddell requires of me."

"This is wrong—to make me the instrument of Lord Lyddell's anger toward the boy."

"That may be true, but orders are orders. He's your responsibility until he repents." With that, Graves turned and marched back across the courtyard to the kitchen.

John turned to Joshua. "Well, you've certainly put me in a fix, young man."

"I'm sorry about that, sir."

"If you don't like the way you're being treated, then you have the power to change that way." He pointed at the servant's entrance. "You heard Mister Graves. You were brought here to be raised as a gifted child. Do you know what that is worth? Do you have any idea what most every other child in England would give in exchange for what you have been offered?"

"I didn't ask for this!"

"Well, I have no sympathy for you, Thomas Flint!"

"That's not my name!"

John lowered his voice and looked again to make certain Graves was gone. "Joshua Smoot has made himself a slave—to do the filthy and cruel work that

Ned does every day. Thomas Flint, on the other hand, has the power to escape that toil by simply changing his name."

"Wait!" Ned spread his arms and looked about. "If he does *my* work, then what am I to do?"

"You, young man, have just been promoted."

"I get to ride the horses?"

"Aye, and then I'll have more time for my reading."

Joshua looked to the stables. "I've never been on a horse."

"And you never will as Joshua Smoot." John pointed to the double doors. "The closest you'll get to riding one is when you lead them from the stalls so you can muck their dung and take it to the gardener." With that, John turned and walked to the stables.

Ned helped Joshua up. "This is some mess you've brought on yourself."

Joshua tried to wipe the mud from his clothes. "I don't belong here."

"Neither do I, but there's nowhere else for an eight-year-old *orphaned bastard* to go."

"You too?"

"Yes. My mother was a prostitute and died when I was four. She didn't know who my father was."

"I had a home, a mother, and a sister in Savannah. She taught me and my sister to read, write, and do our sums. John Flint killed my mother and brought me here on his pirate ship."

"Joshua Smoot is a fool." Ned gave him a rough push. "I would trade places with you and take any name they want to put on me."

"Never!"

☠ ☠ ☠

The stable was long and narrow, with four stalls on one wall and six on the other. A second set of double doors led to a large paddock where two horses were pulling at the fresh grass that grew around the fence posts.

John stepped into the first empty stall and pointed at the trough. "First thing every morning, your job will be to drain, scrub, and fill every watering trough, including the two outside."

"That's all? Just drain and fill them?"

"You didn't hear me. After you drain each one, you use a brush and scrub them clean."

"Every day?"

"Our horses never get sick because their food and water are kept clean." John pointed outside. "You have other jobs, Thomas."

"Don't call me that! My name is Joshua—Joshua Smoot."

"And my name is King George!" Ned gave Joshua a push. "Get used to it, *Thomas Flint*." Ned walked away to the stable and stood next to one of the outside water troughs. "Come here!"

"What?"

"First you pull the plug on one watering trough at a time, scrub it out with that brush on the hook, put the plug back in, and then fill it up with this bucket." He pointed toward the kitchen door. "You get the water from the cistern over there."

"By myself?" Joshua looked around the stable at the other troughs. "How many are there?"

"Twelve, and I've been doing it by myself for over three years!" Ned took Joshua back to the trough he had just drained. "Too complicated for you?"

"No."

Ned squeezed Joshua's upper arm. "You're strong enough to carry a bucket of water, aren't you?"

Joshua looked up at the mansion. "I had my own bed in Savannah." He turned to Ned. "Where will I sleep?"

Ned pointed to a cottage beyond the stables. "With John and me I suppose."

John stepped from the stable. "Not so fast, Ned." John turned to Joshua. "You heard Mister Graves. You will sleep in the stables until you can stand before Lord Lyddell and confess the name of Thomas Flint. Why not do it now and save us all a lot of trouble?"

Joshua turned and looked up at the dower gray stone edifice. The ivy, that had not died and fallen away from the mortar like burial rags, covered most of the house. He looked back at John. "Would you change your name to live in that big house?"

"Of course, I would, but nobody cares that I'm named John Manley."

"But it's not my name, and if you call me by that name, I will not work."

"You heard Graves. If I call you by your real name, I could be sacked without a reference."

"Then what will we call him?" Ned circled Joshua and rubbed his chin the same way John did when he was trying to solve a riddle. "We get sacked if we call him Joshua Smoot, and he refuses to work if we call him Thomas Flint. How about we call him by the chores he does?"

Joshua looked at Ned. "What? Waterboy?"

"Ha!" Ned gave a laugh. "We should call you Dung Boy, because that's what you'll do the rest of the day after the troughs are filled."

Joshua gave Ned an angry look and turned to John. "Ben Gunn and some of the crew on the *Walrus* called me Laddy."

"Well, it's not a proper name by a long shot, but I think it will do."

"I like Dung Boy better, but I suppose Laddy will do." Ned grabbed Joshua's arm. "Come with me, *Laddy*, and I'll show you how to do your first chore."

Joshua resisted and looked to John. "Can I ask a favor first?"

"Of course, as long as it doesn't keep you from your chores."

"I haven't eaten in two days. Do you have any food?"

Ned turned and ran toward the cottage. "Come on!" Once inside, he took Joshua to the hearth where a large kettle hung on a swivel arm. He pulled it away from the coals with the ladle. "It's not fresh, but there's everything in it you'd want."

Joshua breathed in the inviting aroma and nodded. "Right now, I'd eat a bilge rat if it was cooked."

"Well then." Ned handed Joshua a bowl and the ladle. "John's stew is a far better meal than any rat I've ever eaten." He laughed. "If you like the meat, you can thank me because I trapped it."

John stepped to the door. "Are you bad-mouthing my stew, Ned?"

Ned turned. "No—never. I was just telling Laddy that he can thank me for the meat." He pointed into the pot. "Mostly rabbit and a little crow."

Joshua took a large bite and looked at Ned. "How do you catch them?"

Ned stepped to the ladder. "I'll show you." In a moment, Ned climbed up to his loft. He held out a long bow and a quiver of arrows. "I trap most of the rabbits with horse tail snares, but I have to shoot down the birds."

Joshua swallowed. "Will you teach me?"

"Sure, Laddy." He gave a wink and a nudge. "And I'll teach you how to poach without getting caught, and in exchange, you can teach me to read and do my sums."

John took a seat next to Joshua. "I just had a thought." Both Joshua and Ned looked about. "We three know why Lord Lyddell and Mister Graves have put you here. He wants you broken." The boys nodded. "We can give them that illusion while keeping my employment safe while making life good for the three of us."

Ned gave a tilt of his head. "How?"

"Graves is nobody's fool. He'll be watching closely and making regular reports to Lyddell."

Ned jumped up and grabbed a Hickory stick that stood in the corner. "You could give him a beating in the courtyard like you used to do to me. They'd love to watch that."

"Aye." John smiled. "Do you still have those feed bags I sewed together?"

Ned pointed up at his loft. "Aye—just in case we needed to give the master and his butler another show."

Joshua looked from Ned to John. "It sounds like you two have done this before."

John put a hand on Ned's shoulder. "Sometimes you have to give people what they want."

While Joshua finished his second bowl of stew, Ned climbed back up to the loft and called down to John. "They're in the library with the window pushed open, and they're watching the courtyard. I know it's early, John, but this might be just the time to give Laddy his first beating." Ned dropped down and brought the sewn feed bags to John. "Here."

John took the garment. "Take off your shirt and slip your arms through these loops."

While Joshua slipped the half inch layer of bags on, Ned picked up the water bucket and threw it out through the door into the courtyard. "There! I'll run out and grab the bucket while you drag Joshua to the cart for his beating."

A moment later, John pulled Joshua kicking and screaming from the cottage. With several pieces of twine, he and Ned tied Joshua prone over a hand cart. "One last time, Thomas Flint! Will you obey my orders?"

"No, not until you call me by my real name!"

"Then tell me your name!"

"I'm Joshua Smoot, and I will always be Joshua Smoot!"

With that, John delivered three blows to Joshua's back while Ned danced about the cart and mocked the screaming boy. "Ask him again!"

"Tell me your name!"

"My name is Joshua Smoot!'

John commenced beating Joshua's back again, and only stopped when Ned quit circling the cart and yelled. "Stop, John! He's senseless, and you might have killed him!"

"Nobody dies with only a dozen stripes." John pointed to the bucket. "Douse him with water."

Ned was back a moment later and threw the water over Joshua's head.

"Ah!" Joshua jerked awake. "My name is still Joshua Smoot!"

"No, it will be Dung Boy until you repent." John threw down the stick. "Take him to the stable, and after he's recovered, put him to work."

High in the mansion library, Graves stepped next to his master. "Ha! They've named him Dung Boy."

"Young Thomas just found out that he doesn't have a single friend at Wakehurst Place." Lyddell looked to Graves. "We can expect young Thomas back inside by dinner time."

☠ ☠ ☠

When the mock beating was complete, John left Joshua tied to the cart for nearly an hour. Finally, after Ned had berated Joshua long enough for refusing his name, he untied him, leaned close and whispered. "How was that, Laddy?"

"I will take a beating like that every day if you and John think it will fool them."

"Well, maybe once or twice a week—just enough to convince them that John is a cruel taskmaster and that I hate you."

"I still refuse to take that name, Ned."

"That's up to you, Laddy." He picked up the bucket and handed it to Joshua. "John tells me that many years ago when Wakehurst was being planned that the kitchen was built over a spring that pushes water up into several of these cisterns about the estate." He pointed to the garden and the orchard beyond. "The gardener gets his water from that cistern just beyond that stone wall."

Joshua turned and pointed to the entrance road. "Why can't the horses drink water from that stream that flows under the bridge?"

"John said that the horses sometimes got sick from that water—that there's no telling what kind of bugs or parasites come down from the uplands."

By midday, all the troughs were emptied, scrubbed, and refilled, and Joshua was now hard at work mucking out the stalls. As he was dumping the first load of manure on the dung pile behind the stables, a man called to him from several spans away.

"So, you're Thomas Flint!" It was a large man who spoke with a thickness of speech as if his mouth was full of food. Joshua looked at the man for a long moment and then turned the cart about and started back for the stables. "Hey!" The man stepped to Joshua and grabbed him roughly by the shoulder. "You'll answer me when I address you, or you'll get my backhand on top of that beating you just took!"

"What do you want?"

"I know everything about you."

"How can you know anything about me?" Joshua looked up at the morning sun. "I was only brought here during the night and thrown outside two hours ago."

"I know because Jenny—the maid who washed and dressed you for the breakfast you turned down—is my daughter. She told me everything that happened this morning."

"What did she tell you?"

"She told me that you're a rich brat from Savannah who doesn't like his new name, so the master's making you work in the stables until you do."

"Is that all?"

"She also told me that Lord Lyddell and the butler are having a hoot over John Manley calling you Dung Boy."

Joshua studied the man. "Who are you?"

"I'm Jacob." He turned and pointed at the grounds. "My last name is Gardner. Me and my four other daughters tend the gardens, the orchards, and the rest of the grounds here at Wakehurst Place."

"Did Lyddell make you take that name?"

"No. The name has been in my family for generations."

"Are you a slave?"

"A slave?" The man gave a laugh, surprised at the boy's ignorance. "I'm a domestic, which means that I'm a free man and I'm here by my own choice."

"A domestic? I have heard that word before, and I think it's just another word for slave."

"What could a rich child like you know about slaves?"

"I saw slaves in Savannah—black slaves and white slaves but for vanity's sake, their masters called them indentured servants."

"Then why are you here, and why has Lord Lyddell agreed to raise you as if you are his own son?"

I am John Flint's bastard. Lord Lyddell has been forced to take me in to pay back a debt he owed Flint. Part of the debt is that I agree to change my name to Thomas Flint."

"Then it is all about your name."

"Flint killed my mother the day he kidnapped me."

"Why did he kill your mother?"

"See, you don't know as much about me as you think."

"What did she do to him?"

"Her name was Emily Smoot and she was one of Savannah's three midwives. According to Flint, she lied to him about me—that I was a girl and that

I died when I was born—so that he would not make me a pirate. When he discovered that I was a boy and still alive, he killed her and forced my sister and me to watch."

"Then you're not a rich brat like Jenny told us."

"And you're not a slave like the indentured servants in Savannah."

"Well?" The question took the large man back for a moment. He scratched his head, looked around at the garden, and then back to the boy. "My people have served the Lyddell family through many generations. They allow us to live on the land and to take our sustenance from it. In turn, the men fight the master's battles if required." He paused. "But in a way, perhaps Lord Lyddell does own us."

Joshua smiled and offered his hand. "I'm pleased to meet you, Jacob Gardner. My name is Joshua Smoot."

Jacob turned and looked toward the mansion as he took Joshua's hand. "We've been told that if we're caught speaking that name, we'll be put off the land without a letter of reference." He gave the boy a large smile, looked about, and lowered his voice. "Welcome to Wakehurst Place, Joshua Smoot."

"Thank you, Jacob."

"Can you hunt, Joshua?"

"Why?"

"Because we don't get much meat. If you're any good with a longbow, there's no quicker way to make friends with the other domestics than to bring them fresh meat."

"Ned told me that he'd teach me."

"I have a long bow and a dozen or so arrows that I don't use any more. I was hoping that one of my girls would be born a boy so he could do some hunting for us, but the good Lord didn't see it my way. If you promise to share your game with us, you can have it."

"Yes! And I promise to share my kill with you."

Jacob noticed the curtain move in Lyddell's window. "We're being watched, Joshua." He pointed at the dung cart. "I best get back to my garden and you best get back to mucking the horse stalls."

CHAPTER SIX:
The Brood Mare Emily

J oshua took well to his new life at Wakehurst Place with an enthusi-
asm rarely seen in southern England. He loved the horses and the
various tasks that kept them clean, fed, and in good health, but
against John Manley's advice to never make livestock a pet, he adopted a
brood mare named Emily. Joshua's bed roll had a permanent place on the
fodder in her stall.

Under Ned's guiding hand, Joshua quickly learned the art of trapping
and shooting fowl on the fly, and the weekly game he brought to the various
domestics earned him great favor at Wakehurst Place. By his tenth birthday,
Joshua had become an able archer and trapper in the true tradition of Robin
Hood, and word came often from the kitchen that some of his finer kills found
their way to Lord Lyddell's table.

The mock courtyard beatings had ceased after the first year, but Joshua
continued to reject the name Thomas Flint. Lord Lyddell tired of summoning
Joshua to his room monthly, determined that he would offer the lad redemption only once a year on the anniversary of his arrival.

The years passed quickly, and Joshua grew from the spindly eight-year-
old to a strapping young man who rivaled John Flint in physical strength and
agility.

The Lord of Wakehurst Place sat alone at his bedroom window looking
down upon the strong-willed young man carrying the buckets of water from
the cistern to the stables. But now, instead of a single bucket filled half way,
the eighteen-year-old carried two full buckets at a time. The battle of wills had
consumed Lyddell's spirit and was beginning to threaten his physical health as
well.

"Sir?"

"What?" Charles would not look away from the courtyard and the stables
beyond. Graves knew this day was difficult for his master, but his instructions
were clear. This was the tenth anniversary of the day John Flint had delivered
the boy to the Brighton dock. "Shall I summon the lad?"

"He's beat me, Graves."

"No, he hasn't, sir." Graves stepped to the frail man and took the blood-soaked handkerchief from his hand, replacing it with a freshly laundered one. "Perhaps ten years has been enough of hard labor in the stables. Perhaps it will be this year that the lad repents of his stubbornness."

"Enough?" Lyddell gave a slow shake of his head. "I took John Flint's money. I signed that blood covenant. I gave my assurance that I would succeed at my task, but I have failed—utterly failed."

"No." The butler folded the soiled piece of cloth carefully, so as not to get any of the blood on himself. "It is the lad who has failed. He could have had the world, but he refused to claim his birthright."

Charles turned back to the courtyard and watched for a long moment. "But he—"

"He could have lived in the house with the clean linens and fresh clothing, sir. He could have eaten at your table. He could have completed his formal education and chosen a vocation by now. It is his stubbornness that has denied him those opportunities and chained him to the stables. You have not lost, sir, unless—"

"Look!" Charles held up a bundle of letters. "These are John Flint's letters to me—one sent each year. I've been turned into a liar—telling him that young Thomas is progressing wonderfully. Lord willing, I will die of this consumption before John Flint runs me through with his cutlass and eats my heart."

"Forgive me for this, but since you mentioned eating, you need to eat something, and you also need to get out of this room."

"I have no will for it, Graves. I..." His voice trailed off as a fit of coughing engulfed him.

"You used to ride, sir. You used to hunt pheasant with your friends." Graves walked to the window and pulled the curtain aside. "Now all you do is obsess over that boy." He turned back to his master. "If it would help...if it would get you up again...perhaps you should admit to him that he has won."

There was a light knock at the open door. Whoever it was remained in the hall, just out of sight.

"Is that him?" Charles turned and looked at the door. Graves set the master's dinner on the sideboard and stepped to the door. "We expected Thomas." Graves lowered his voice. "Why are you here, Manley?"

Charles called again. "Is it him?"

"It's the stable master, sir."

"What does *he* want?"

"I'll ask, sir." Graves put a finger to his lips, leaned close, and touched his ear.

"Well?" Charles was choked by another string of coughs while Manley whispered his message. Graves straightened and turned. "It's not about Thomas, sir."

"Then why in God's name is he here instead of Thomas?"

John stepped into the doorway. "It's one of the brood mares, sir. She has the equine cough. I need your permission to go to the village for the medication she needs."

"Which one?" Charles gripped the drapes for support and pointed down at the horse standing in the courtyard. "Is that the one?"

John stepped to the window and nodded. "It's Emily, sir."

"Young Thomas likes that old mare, doesn't he?"

"I…" John faltered.

"Out with it, man! Emily is his favorite, isn't she?"

"Begging your pardon, sir, but the lad…Thomas…likes *all* the running stock."

"But he likes *that one* a little more than the rest because that was his mother's name, right?"

"That was his mother's name sir but he'd—"

"No!" Charles turned back to the window. "You may not purchase any medicine for that mare!"

"But she's carrying a foal that has an excellent blood line, and the medicine would only cost you shillings—"

"I want her to die."

"But…" John retreated a step from his master.

Charles released the drape and turned on the man. "Tell Thomas that this is the last time I'll offer my kindness! Tell him that unless he takes his rightful name—the name John Flint has given him—that his pet mare will be allowed to die of her disease, and that it will be his fault."

"It means *that much* to you, sir? You would kill one of your best brood mares—"

"Yes! It means *that much* to me!"

"But the mare, sir. It's not her fault, any more than it was my fault when you assigned the lad's punishment to me."

Charles simmered for a long moment. "You have my decision regarding Emily the brood mare. I'll leave it to you to convince the lad to stand before me and repent."

"Don't do this, sir!" John twisted his hat. "The mare has several more productive years in her, and her pedigree is strong. You'll regret this decision, sir."

"Enough!" Charles turned away to the window. "Leave me!"

Graves gave John a nod toward the hallway. "Tell the boy to scrub up and then bring him here just after lunch."

John backed to the door, gave a slow shake of his head, and was gone.

☠ ☠ ☠

"I'll kill him!" Joshua looked up at Lyddell's window. "He and my father know nothing but killing, so that's what I'll give him!"

"No, you won't." John went to a panel in the stable and brought back a metal tin. "I have some money saved up. I'll pay for the medicine myself."

Joshua turned back to John. "Up until now, it's been a game between us. He calls me into the house once a year and asks if I've repented. I tell him my name is still Joshua Smoot. He points to the door and I leave."

"Well, now that he's threatened Emily's life, you know how serious he is."

"Flint did this with Ben Gunn a dozen days out of Savannah. He threatened to kill Ben and eat his heart if I didn't change my name."

"He didn't kill Ben, did he?"

"No. That was only a bluff to scare me."

"Ben Gunn was a man. Emily is just a horse."

CHAPTER SEVEN:
Joshua's Escape

Since he had fallen ill with consumption, Charles Lyddell had made it his practice to take his meals in his bedroom. Graves was just taking the lunch tray away as Joshua stepped to the door. Graves stopped and glared at the young man. "You!"

"Who's there, Graves?" Lord Lyddell gave a cough and turned. "Is it him?"

"It's me—Joshua Smoot!" He pushed Graves aside and strode to the sick man's bed. The boy stood six feet tall and weighed 180 pounds. His features were nothing like his father's. Even though he was angry, there was a certain kindness to his eyes that spoke of good breeding. Joshua's hair hung to his shoulders in light brown curls.

"Well—evidently you've decided that the brood mare's life is more important than your name."

"You already know my answer."

"Before you say something that you'll regret, I want you to know I've reconsidered."

"Reconsidered what?"

"I have decided that I will not allow the virus to kill your pet horse Emily." Joshua gave his master a narrow look. "That surprises you, doesn't it?"

"Yes, considering—"

"But her life is still in your hands, Thomas. She will live or die by the decision you make in the next minute."

"But you just said she won't die."

"Wrong! I said the virus would not kill her."

It took Joshua only a moment to realize what his master was saying. He shook his head slowly from side to side.

"Are you certain?"

Joshua nodded.

"I want to hear the words!"

"My name is Joshua Smoot! I will never take the name that my murdering father gave me!"

"Very well." Charles looked at Joshua for a long moment. "The brood mare, Emily, will be put down in the morning at first light. Her flesh will be stripped from her bones and she shall be roasted for my dinner! I will eat her until I have consumed—"

Before Charles could finish, Joshua leaped onto the bed. "You'll burn in hell!" Joshua wrapped his fingers about the man's throat and squeezed with all his might. With each gasp, blood spewed from between the old man's teeth. Joshua did not remember anything after that, except the momentary sound of someone running behind him, and something hitting his head.

When Joshua awoke, it was to darkness. He lay on a cold and wet stone floor surrounded by coal. With an effort, he pushed himself up onto his knees, rubbed the back of his head, and looked around. "The coal room." There was a single barred window high on the stone wall. The moon was full and it was a clear night, but something was blocking the sky. Joshua walked toward the light.

"He's awake!" It was Ned. "Now!"

Joshua moved closer. "Ned! What happened?"

There was a momentary sound of ropes pulling taught, followed by breaking rock and metal being wrenched free. A lantern was thrust through the opening in the wall, illuminating the temporary dungeon.

"Over here, Joshua!" A voice came through the settling dust. "Take my hand!"

"What happened, Ned?" Joshua took the offered hand. "Did I kill him?"

"There isn't time! Quick!"

A moment later, Joshua was pulled through the rough hole and out onto the courtyard near the cistern. He reached down and felt the tops of his feet. Each one was rubbed raw and bleeding. "My feet! What did they do to me?"

"They dragged you from Lord Lyddell's bedroom, down the stairs, through the kitchen, and locked you in the coal room. It would have helped if you were wearing your shoes."

"I was choking Lyddell, and then somebody hit me!"

Ned pulled him across the cobblestones toward the stables. "We have everything you need tied onto Emily's back! Can you ride?"

Joshua pulled free. "I think so but—"

"This is no time to be stubborn, Laddy!" Ned spun behind Joshua and pushed him forward. "John knows of a place of refuge where you can go!"

"Where?"

"It's several hours north from here toward Lambeth. I have never been there, but it sounds to be perfect!"

At the stables, John pulled the collar and ropes from Emily's neck and began tying a large bundle to her back. Joshua's long bow and quiver of arrows was draped over the right side.

"How is he, Ned?" John finished the last hitch and looked around at the two teens. "Can he ride?"

"Yes, but he's still confused."

"We thought you were dead, Laddy." John gave the load a jerk to make sure it was secure. "Graves hit you across the back of the head several times with a candlestick!"

"Is he still planning to put Emily down tomorrow?"

"Aye, and that's the only reason you're still alive. Lyddell had you locked in the coal room because he wanted everyone to see you watch her being killed and slaughtered."

"Ned says there's a place toward Lambeth where I can take her."

John pulled a crude map from his apron and spread it on the workbench next to the lamp. "There's a large lake to the northeast called Weir Wood. It's a two-hour ride."

"Yes?"

"On the northern edge near the far end of the lake is a closed canyon with a single narrow entrance. The entrance is turned sideways so it's invisible unless you know that it's there. A spring-fed stream issues from its upper end, runs out through the entrance, and down to the lake." He touched the small drawing at the corner. "Look for the stream and you'll find the entrance."

"How long do you think Emily and I will have to hide there?"

John gave Joshua a long look. "You can never come back, Laddy. There'll be a King's warrant on your head for attempted murder, and once they know you took Emily, there will be a second warrant for horse thievery. Those are both hanging offenses."

Joshua looked down at the map. "Tell me more about this canyon."

"It's on the Carlisle Estate, but I don't think anybody ever goes there. There should be plenty of water and grass for the mare. We've packed your longbow and arrows, all your traps, your flint and a cooking pot, our bedding—everything you'll need."

Ned climbed up the ladder to the loft and called down. "There's no telling how long you'll have to live out there, Laddy!" John and Joshua could hear him rummaging around, and then a bundle of clothes flew over the rail and landed between the two. Ned looked over the rail. "You'll need extra clothes. We're the same size, so all of that should fit."

John turned to Joshua. "They must have heard the wall breaking, so they'll know you've escaped. You must leave now!" John stepped close and wrapping his arms about the young man. "You realize, of course, that we'll probably never see one another again."

Joshua hugged the old man with all his strength. "You've been the only father I've ever known, John. Someday—somehow—I'll honor your name."

"It's enough to know you're safe from Wakehurst Place and Charles Lyddell." John took something from his waist pocket and held it out to Joshua. "Take this."

"What is it?"

John moved his hand into the beam of light from the small lantern. "It's a ring."

Joshua took the shiny circle of metal.

"It's only a polished Ferrier's nail, but it would mean a lot to me if you'd wear it."

Joshua pushed it onto his finger and looked up. "Thank you, John. This means more to me than you know."

Tears streamed down John's cheeks. "Go now, Laddy, and remember the story I told you about Lot and his wife. Ride hard and don't look back at this God-awful place."

Joshua jumped onto Emily's back. "Before I go, John, there's one more thing."

"Yes?"

"My name! Would you call me by my real name just once before I go?"

John wiped the tears from his cheeks and then saluted. "Goodbye, my son. Goodbye, Joshua Smoot."

☠ ☠ ☠

Graves was winded when he reached the third floor and let himself into his master's bedroom. "Sir?"

"I'm awake." Charles sat up. "What is it?"

"They're gone."

"Who's gone?" Charles threw back the blankets, swung his legs to the floor, and got out of bed.

"There's a four-foot hole in the coal room wall just beyond the cistern, and both Thomas and the brood mare are gone."

"The stable master and that damn orphan must have done this."

"Definitely, sir." Graves nodded. "They both claim that they didn't hear or see anything, but I know the two helped him escape. The bars on the coal room were strong—more than one man could break, even young Thomas. Shall I notify the constable?"

"Yes, and have Manley prepare my carriage. Tell him that I need to ride to Ardingly to see my doctor."

"Is it your lungs, sir?" Graves offered his master a housecoat. "More blood?"

Charles pushed Graves away. "That's not why I'm going to Ardingly."

"Then…?"

"Tell John Manley that Ned is to accompany us to help my footmen get me in and out of the carriage." Charles pushed into his slippers, stood, and stepped to the window. The courtyard and stable were still dark. "It will be a special pleasure to deliver those two to the constable."

☠ ☠ ☠

Long before the eastern sky began to turn pink, Joshua had passed the Highblock Estate and had intercepted the trail that led north through Sharpthorn. A quarter mile beyond the small hamlet, he came to a game trail that only a hunter would recognize. He looked at the map and then turned Emily east, into the woods. Within minutes, he guided her through a meadow and into a stand of Willows. Emily's cough had become worse from the strain of the trip, and Joshua intended that she rest. She seemed to recognize his kindness.

Joshua dismounted and walked through the trees toward the sound of several ducks. It was still dark. "The lake!" He ran back to Emily. "We're close. Another hour at the most and we'll be safe."

After a much-needed drink, they were moving again along the edge of the lake. A flock of Mergansers and a single Loon took to the air as they passed close to the shore. A hundred yards further along, Joshua reined up Emily to watch a family of otters frolicking about a partially sunken log. One of the larger animals had a fish, and the others chased him for their share.

Just beyond the fourth stand of willows, Emily stepped into a shallow and rocky brook that cut across their path. Joshua pulled the map from his shirt and held it up to the glow of the morning sun. "This must be it, girl!" He jumped to the ground and led her up the meandering stream for a hundred yards to a stony cliff face that pushed up into the sky fifty feet above the surrounding terrain. The dark grey rock looked to be of shale or flint, and as if it had been tilted up in great chards and then worn down by the rains. The moss and sword ferns had long ago made the dark crevasses their home, giving the structure the appearance of an abandoned medieval castle.

Joshua stopped Emily twenty feet from the rock and looked right and left. "John said the opening would be right here." As if answering his question, Emily lowered her head and took another drink from the stream of water. Joshua looked down to where it emerged ten yards to his left from under a growth of water cress. He pulled her forward.

The entrance to the canyon was just as John had said it would be—narrow and turned to the side. Joshua tied Emily to a tree. On foot, he entered the passage and followed it in a serpentine pattern for nearly twenty feet before it opened into an enclosed canyon that was in the general shape of a lima bean. By his best estimate, it measured thirty yards long and twenty yards wide with the stream cutting through the center of a carpet of several varieties of fresh flowers Joshua had seen in the gardens surrounding Wakehurst Place. There were roses, geraniums, heather, and several other common garden plants and vegetables, all covered with a thick layer of dew. Joshua returned to Emily and led her inside where she immediately began munching at a tall rose bush.

"This is incredible!" Joshua turned about to survey his new home. All four sides of the canyon were solid rock. As he turned about, something on the north wall caught his eye. He walked along the stream to where it emerged from a low irregular-shaped cave with an entrance ten feet high and six feet wide. The spring bubbled up in a pool to the right of the entrance and then spilled out and across the canyon. Joshua stepped inside and waited for his eyes to adjust.

The cave was perfect. Once beyond the entrance, it opened into a large room that measured three spans wide and long. Joshua stepped back outside and looked at the bundle on Emily's back. "You have to see this, Emily. It's big enough for both of us."

Joshua's first task was to find enough branches to fashion a gate that would keep Emily from wandering from the canyon. By mid-morning, he stood back to survey his work. Fortunately, John and Ned had supplied him with a lantern and plenty of whale oil, a small faller's ax, a set of fire irons, and a month's supply of grain. There were also four steel traps, his longbow, and two-dozen arrows. He found a flat spot and spread his bed roll out, cross-wise near the deepest wall of the cave.

Long before mid-day, Joshua had set out his traps along the lake shore where it was obvious that the animals came to drink and hunt. With an apology to Emily, he cut ten hairs from her tail and tied snares to spread along the small game trails that covered the meadows. Before the sun had finally set upon this first of many days as a fugitive of the King, he had already snared three partridges for dinner. So as not to over hunt the area, he collected the metal traps and turned back toward the canyon. As he approached the entrance, he heard the noise of cracking twigs to the west. He froze, and carefully knocked an arrow onto his longbow. There was another sound, this time much louder than the first.

"It has to be a stag." He crept toward the sound and peered through the thick growth of trees. A movement caught his eye. He brought the bow up and stepped into the open.

"Emily!" He lowered the bow and put the arrow back in his quiver. "By John Flint's black heart, what are you doing outside the canyon?" The mare raised her head and gave him a huff. He pointed at the canyon entrance. "You have all those flowers and that fresh water, but you would rather be out here, eating these weeds?" He pulled the doubled length of rope from his trousers, tied a makeshift halter, and threw it over her head.

"You're not well, you know." He checked his knot and pulled the mare back to the narrow entrance. Several feet inside, he stopped and pointed behind Emily. "It's cold and windy out there! And besides, how did you manage to push away this gate?"

She did not share his concern, so he led her the rest of the way through the passage and out into the secluded canyon. Joshua removed the halter and then returned to replace the barrier. As he reached for the first branch, there was a scream that sounded like a large cat. Before Joshua could turn, the thing leaped onto his back and knocked him to the ground.

CHAPTER EIGHT:
The Secret Garden

Whatever it was that had attacked him, Joshua was thrown forward, face into the mud. As the thing tore at his neck and hair, Joshua gathered all his strength and gave one mighty push upward. The thing was thrown aside long enough for Joshua to jump to his feet. He whirled about, stumbled against the rocks, turned around, and searched for the thing.

As quickly as the thing had attacked, it was gone. He pulled his knife from his belt, ran out into the open canyon. There was no sign of the beast—only the waist-deep flowers and the tranquil sound of the stream bubbling past.

Joshua lowered his body and crept forward toward Emily, figuring that if the thing was hungry, it might attack her next. "Where is it, Emily?" His keen eyes scanned the canyon. "Where did it go?"

As he approached to within three spans of the mare, there was a sound to his right. He turned just in time to catch a walnut-sized rock square in the middle of his forehead. For the second time in a day, he was knocked unconscious.

He could not tell how long he had been senseless, but when he finally awoke, his hands were tied behind his back, and there was a knife pressed against his throat "Who are you and what are you doing in my garden?"

Everything was a blur. Joshua blinked and tried to reach up to his face. "My hands!"

"Tell me who you are or I'll slit your throat and leave you here to bleed out and rot!"

"My name is Joshua Smoot. I—"

"Your horse is eating my flowers, Joshua Smoot, and from the looks of it, you've taken up housekeeping in my cave!"

"*Your cave?*"

"This is the Weir Wood Reservoir, and it's on Lord Carlisle's estate. You are a trespasser."

Joshua blinked again. The voice was angry, but it was a girl's voice. His eyes finally focused on blue eyes, long blonde hair, and a light-yellow dress. "Who are you?"

"My name is Rebecca Keyes. This is my garden."

"Nice to meet you, Rebecca Keyes."

"Right!" She kept the knife at his throat. "We know each other's names, but you still haven't told me why you and your horse are here."

"I'm..." He gave a frustrated huff. "It's a very long story. I don't think you have time for it."

"If that's the way you want it, I'll just cut your throat now and be done with you!" She leaned down and pressed the knife harder against his skin. "Too bad you have to die. You're not half bad on the eyes, Joshua Smoot."

"Wait! I'm a runaway from Wakehurst Place to the south. Lord Lyddell was going to kill my horse in front of the staff and families that work the estate, and then serve her up for dinner."

"Oh?" Rebecca turned and looked around at Emily. "Why would he do such a thing?"

"Because she's my favorite horse and he hates me." While he spoke, Joshua worked his hands back and forth until the knot released. "She has equine cough and I asked for medication."

"Why does he hate you?"

"Because I won't change my name." Joshua had had enough horse play. With one enormous push with his hips and arms, the girl flew into the air and landed on her face in the heather. Before she could flip over, Joshua was on her back and had wrenched the knife from her hand.

"This is better." Joshua held her fast. "Now, if you promise to behave your-self, I'll let you turn over."

"No! This is my garden!" She twisted her head sideways and spit out the plants. "Take your horse and go away!"

"If we go back, it will be a noose for me and Emily will be slaughtered."

"Okay!" She stopped struggling. "Let me up!"

"Not until you promise to behave yourself, and then I'm only going to let you turn onto your back."

"Fine!" She took several seconds to decide. "I promise to behave myself!"

Joshua eased his grip enough to allow her to twist over. She was dirty, but Joshua had never seen such a beautiful face. Her hair was the color of wheat, and her eyes were as blue as the sky on a clear day. She was much smaller than he was but physically mature.

"Well, Rebecca Keyes, now it's your turn. What is your claim to this canyon?"

"It's a garden, and it's mine because I'm the only one who knows about it. I planted all those flowers your mare is eating!" She struggled to free her arms.

He tightened his grip. "Do you have more than a finder's claim to it?"

"What's *that* supposed to mean?"

He looked at her clothing. It was the typical farm girl's dress and apron. "You're not a member of Lord Carlisle's family, are you?"

"That doesn't matter!"

"Ha! You *are* just like me. A trespasser."

"But I found the garden first, so that gives me what you said—a finder's claim to it!"

"Well, I've found it too, and because I need it more than you, it is now mine."

"What makes you more needful than me?"

"Have you ever heard of the pirate Captain John Flint?" She shook her head. "I'm his bastard son." He held up his right palm to her. "He killed my mother while I watched, and he did this to me."

She took his hand, turned it over, and looked at the scar on the back. "Did he nail you to a tree like they did to Jesus?"

"He threw a pike pole at me as I was being dragged into the sea by the chain he'd fastened to my ankle."

It took her a moment. "So, was he trying to kill you with the pike, or save you from drowning?"

"I was told it was to kill me, but I'll never know for sure—not unless he tells me some day."

"If you're a pirate's bastard, then what are you doing in England so far from the sea?"

"I'm his only son, and he called due a huge debt to force Lord Lyddell to take me in and raise me as a gentleman."

"From the looks of you, it didn't take very well."

"Everything was conditioned on me taking the name John Flint chose for me. That was ten years ago. Once every year since, Lyddell and I have played our parts in the same silly ritual. He would ask if I have repented and decided to become Thomas Flint, and I would tell him that my name is Joshua Smoot. Then he would send me back to the stables."

She studied him for a moment. "All for a name?" Joshua nodded. "I'm the third daughter of a farmer—a man who cares for Lord Carlisle's crops. If I was offered what you were, and the only price was that I had to change my name, they could have called me Helen Highwater or Mary Christmas and I would have agreed."

"There's more. When Captain Flint kidnapped me from Savannah, he shot my mother in the face in front of me."

Just then, Emily coughed. "You're right about your horse. She needs medication."

Joshua shook his head. "I was hoping that she might get better here."

"If you'll let me up, I promise I won't try to kill you anymore."

"Why should I trust you?"

"Our stable master has the medicine she needs. Let me up and I promise I'll cure your horse."

"I also need your promise that Emily and I can stay here, and that you won't tell anybody about us."

"Why?"

"There will be two King's warrants for my head—one for attacking Lord Lyddell, and one for stealing Emily."

It took her a moment. "Alright—I promise."

With a smile, he leaned down toward her face.

She turned her face to the side. "What?"

"A kiss."

"What for?"

"To seal our agreement."

"That's three agreements." She blinked several times and gave him a smirk. "Are you asking me for three kisses?"

He smiled. "This one's for Emily and her medicine." He bent down and touched his lips to hers. It was a light kiss, like a butterfly landing on a flower. When their lips parted, he opened his eyes and then she opened hers. She gave a quiet sigh.

"This is for letting us stay in your garden."

She closed her eyes as their lips met for the second time. The kiss was stronger than the first and lasted several seconds. Rebecca's pulse raced and her breaths came faster. She opened her eyes and looked longingly into his. "Before we seal the third promise, can I get up?" Joshua released her arms and helped her to sit up. "My garden's already a secret, so nobody will ever know about you or your mare." The third kiss was longer and more passionate than the first two. Rebecca finally pushed back and looked at Joshua. "I'm not the first girl you've kissed, am I?"

"The girls at Wakehurst traded kisses for the game I brought them, and I'm sure those weren't your first kisses either."

They both laughed, and then Emily coughed.

"How long has she been like that?"

Joshua stood and helped her to her feet. "Three or four days, and she's not getting better."

"One of our geldings had the same thing last month. That's why we have the medicine."

"Did he die?"

Rebecca shook her head and then looked up at the fog that hung over the canyon. "It's still early. I could be back with the medicine she needs before dusk."

"Did you come by foot?"

"Do I look like I could afford a horse?"

"No." He pointed at Emily. "I'm sure she's strong enough to carry both of us to your stables."

"In her condition, the strain could kill her." She pointed. "We'll take her, but you can walk beside her as good as me."

☠ ☠ ☠

Thirty minutes later, the three stopped at the last stand of trees before the Carlisle Estate and tied Emily to a tree. Once the knot was secure, Joshua turned and rained several kisses onto her upturned face.

"What are those kisses for?"

"Who knows?" Joshua gave her another kiss. "Maybe we'll be making a lot more promises someday, so those are like a buried treasure to be dug up when we need them."

"I like the sound of that." With a look to the large estate, she put a hand against his chest. "Wait here."

"Why? Nobody at your estate knows anything about me or the trouble I'm facing."

"No, and they never will if you're careful."

"But what if I want to come to visit you someday?"

"You can never come here."

"But—"

"Lord Lyddell will be issuing those warrants for your arrest, and they will be delivered to all the nearby estates. You can't be seen by anybody." She kissed his lips and backed away a step. "Besides, we agreed that you and my garden are my secret."

"Alright, but please don't be gone too long. I wasn't lonely before, but now that we've met, I'm sure to get lonely the moment you walk away."

She reached up and touched his lips. "Start counting your heart beats. Before you get to a hundred, I'll be back." She pulled him down and gave him a light kiss, turned, and ran away through the knee-high grass. By ten heart beats, she was across the field and onto the roadway that led to the front gate of the estate. He waited for her to look back and wave but she knew better.

"Eight- two, eighty-three…" Joshua stopped at the sound of a twig cracking behind him. He spun about, instinctively pulling his knife.

"You heard me." Rebecca stepped to him, rose on her toes, and gave him a kiss. "I'm usually quieter than that."

"Broken twigs have brought many rabbits and birds to their death." He said, sheathing the knife.

"How high did you count?"

"Eighty-three." Her hands were empty. "Where's the medicine?"

"Wilkins—that's our stable master—wanted to know whose horse I needed it for."

"What did you tell him?"

"I said she was a stray that I found near the lake."

"Will he give you the medicine for a stray?"

"Yes, tomorrow, if…" She gave Joshua a coy smile. "What if the price of the medicine was another kiss?"

"We already kissed for it."

"Wilkins wants a kiss."

"Oh?" Joshua thought. "I suppose your kisses are yours just like mine belong to me. If we have to trade them for things we need, then I guess that's what we must do."

"You wouldn't care if I kissed the stable master to get Emily's medicine?"

"No." Joshua shrugged. "Why should I?"

She stomped her foot. "You're being too understanding."

"But aren't we just friends?"

"Well…yes, I suppose so."

"What if I had to trade a kiss to one of the girls back at Wakehurst for something you needed?" He knew this was getting to her. "You'd understand, wouldn't you?"

"Well…"

"Then you see it?"

"If the thing I needed was as important as Emily's medicine, then, yes, I guess I'd understand you having to kiss another girl for it."

"Well, there you are. If you have to kiss your stable master to save Emily's life, then I'd say it was a good trade."

"Oh!"

"What's the matter?"

"I won't have to kiss him, Joshua." She reached into her apron pocket and pulled out the bottle. "Look here."

"You were testing me, weren't you?"

"I only wanted to know what you would say."

"Did I pass your test?"

"No."

"Why not? What did I do wrong?"

"I wanted you to be jealous for me."

Joshua burst out laughing, pulled her down to the ground on top of him, and showered her with kisses. "There! Emily's medicine is bought and paid for!"

☠ ☠ ☠

Joshua watched the sun climb into the morning sky with the anticipation of a young man in love. His traps were set and he had already checked them twice for game. Emily had eaten her fill of grass and drank the medicated water he had mixed for her. Just as he began stripping the feathers from a grouse, he heard Rebecca's familiar singing from the east. He leaped from the rocks and ran through the trees, meeting Rebecca several hundred feet from the canyon entrance. She carried a young lamb in her arms and had a satchel slung over her shoulder. He showered her face with kisses.

"Glad to see me, huh?" She held out the lamb.

"A peace offering?"

"It's just a lamb, Joshua." She held it up so he could see its left hind leg. "She has a deformed leg and the shepherd was going to put her down if I hadn't begged him for her. I thought that with all the time you spend out here alone that—"

"Accepted!" Joshua reached out and petted the lamb's head. He nodded at the satchel. "What's that?"

"Another gift." He watched while she pulled the satchel from her shoulder and dumped several potatoes, carrots, and other vegetables out onto the grass. She touched the grouse he was carrying. "Emily has eaten most of the vegetables in my garden, so you'll need these things to make a proper stew."

"Thank you." He looked to Emily. "She has already drunk half the water I mixed for her. How long does the medicine take to make her better?"

"It said it on the bottle—two to three days." She gave him a sideways look. "Didn't anybody teach you to read?"

"Of course, I can read." He touched the lamb. "I'm not just another stupid animal."

"I just didn't know whether..." She reached into her apron pocket.

"What else did you bring me?"

She pulled out a worn King James Bible. "The housekeeper gave me this last year when I turned fifteen. I've marked some pages with slips of paper that I want you to read."

He took the Bible. "Before I was kidnapped from Savannah, my mother used to read Bible stories to me and my older sister." He paused. "I miss those times."

"Which stories?"

"Abraham, Moses, Noah and the ark, Jonah and the whale. Stories like that."

"Do you believe them?"

"I used to but not anymore." He looked to the cave. "How long can you stay?"

"Wait."

"What?"

"Why don't you believe those Bible stories anymore?"

"I stopped believing in God the day He let John Flint kill my mother and kidnap me here to England."

"You can't judge God for what evil men do."

"Okay." He took her by the shoulders and tried to pull her close. "You didn't answer me. How long can you stay?"

"An hour or so. I've promised the cook that I would help with dinner."

He gave her a flirtatious raise of his brows. "What shall we do for an hour?"

She pointed to the Bible. "I want you to read those verses I marked."

"But I wanted to kiss you more."

"Hmm." She took several breaths. "I have a proposition for you, Joshua."

"Oh?"

"I'll kiss you once for each verse you memorize."

"Ha! The same as the kisses I got for the fresh meat I brought the girls?"

She pulled the medicine bottle from her apron. "But you said that it's alright to trade kisses for something important."

"Hmm." He gave her a long look, and then got the Bible. "Okay, what do you want me to memorize first?"

"There are ten slips of paper—each with a verse written on it. Those ten first."

He opened to a verse in the Gospel according to John. "I know this one already."

"Which one?"

"Here." He handed her the Bible. "For God so loved the world that He gave His only begotten Son, that whosoever believeth in Him should not perish but have everlasting life." He leaned close. "My kiss?"

"Sure." As he took her into his arms, he slid his hands down past her waist.

"Stop!"

He raised his hands. "It was only a touch."

"An unwelcomed touch, and we both know where that will lead."

Before he could apologize, she marched to the canyon entrance and out into the meadow beyond.

"Wait!"

"No!" She backed away. "You'll make that up to me."

"How?"

"That's up to you, Joshua." She backed further away. "You figure it out."

He followed her outside to the garden. "Another test?"

"Yes!" In a moment, she was gone.

Joshua looked down at his hands. "Damn me!" He returned to the canyon and looked around as if the answer was hiding under a rock or behind a fern. "Ah! I know what she would like!"

The next afternoon, Rebecca walked into the garden with a note in her hand. "Joshua! Where are you?"

"I'm here!" He stepped from the cave, walked across to her, and tried to kiss her. She held her hands out to stop him. "What's the matter Becky?"

"You're trying to make up for trying to take liberties with me, but I want to see what you've done to make amends before I forgive you."

"You're going to love this."

Halfway to the cave, Rebecca stopped and looked about. "Where's the lamb?"

Joshua pointed toward the cave where smoke was rising from the fire. "She's just about ready."

Rebecca followed, not understanding what he was saying. The distinctive smell of cooking lamb filled her nostrils. She stopped and yelled. "You cooked her?"

"Isn't that…?" He looked at the pot and back to her. "You said she was a peace offering."

"No!" She slapped his face. "She was to be your pet. She was to be a companion when I could not be here!"

"I already have Emily."

"She was to be released back to the herd once she was large enough."

She tried to slap him again, but he caught her hand and danced free of her kicks. "Then you should have told me that when you brought her."

"I thought you were smart enough to figure it out." Rebecca pulled free, turned, and walk away toward the canyon entrance.

Joshua grabbed the Bible and followed, catching her arm before she had walked ten paces. "Please don't leave."

She turned. "Those verses you claim you memorized—"

"Claimed?" He held up the Bible. "Are you calling me a liar just so I can kiss you?"

"No, but didn't you learn anything about lambs and sheep—the Bible verses I told you to memorize?"

"Those verses have nothing to do with somebody like me—a person who doesn't believe in God anymore."

"They have everything to do with you. You're just like that lamb you killed and cooked, except you have the opportunity to be saved and go with me to heaven someday."

"That lamb is just food—like a pig or that grouse I was plucking yesterday."

She walked back to the fire and pointed. "God used a lamb to teach us what Jesus did for us on that Roman cross."

"I memorized those verses for kisses." Joshua held the Bible up to her again. "That's what you said I had to do."

"But didn't any of them mean anything to you—the part that said that the wages of sin is death, but the gift of God is eternal life through Jesus Christ our Lord?"

"No! I'm not a sinner and I don't need your God or your Bible." He threw the Bible at her feet.

Rebecca stood for a long moment. "Oh, Joshua." With tears welling in her eyes, she bent down and picked up the sacred book. "God loves you, Joshua. He sent His son, Jesus Christ, as the Lamb of God, to give Himself a sacrifice to take away your sin—your sin, mine, and the sin of the entire world."

Joshua shook his head. "No! God sent John Flint to kill my mother! That's how much your God loves me!"

She stepped to the roasting lamb and stood over it for a moment. "I won't marry a pagan man."

"Who's talking about marriage?"

"Nobody yet, but I just wanted you to know so you would never ask me."

☠ ☠ ☠

It took a full week before Rebecca would speak to Joshua. Twice during that time, he and Emily had gone to the Carlisle estate, but each time, Rebecca sent one of the other women out to him.

"She still doesn't want to see you, Joshua."

Joshua handed the woman a note. "Would you give her this?"

"Only if it's your apology?" She started to unfold it.

"Yes. You can read it if you want."

The woman opened and read the three sentences. She looked up at Joshua and smiled with a mixture of sympathy and longing. "This is nice." She nodded. "I'll have a word with her. Can you wait here for a few minutes?"

"Yes, for as long as it takes her to forgive me."

Ten minutes later, Rebecca came from the kitchen. She carried the note.

"Becky!" He met her at the edge of the roadway. "Please forgive me. I really misunderstood about the lamb and touching you like that. I'll never do anything like that again."

"Then I forgive you."

He touched her hand. "Can we…"

"I have too many chores right now. Come back on Sunday morning while the Lord and Lady Carlisle are away at church."

"Can I kiss you?" Joshua stepped close. "Just one so I know you mean it?"

She smiled and touched his left cheek. "I never stopped loving you, Joshua. That's something you must learn about me—that just because I get angry over something you do; it doesn't mean I don't love you anymore."

He shook his head and touched his chest. "But it hurts in here so much when you're angry with me."

"We'll talk more about this on Sunday."

CHAPTER NINE:
A Fatal Mistake

O ver the next several months, Joshua and Rebecca had changed—
more for her side than for his. For Rebecca, Joshua was an answer
to her prayers. She was certain that she had found the love of her
life—the man who could take her away to a new life. For Joshua, Rebecca
provided a cure for the loneliness that Emily could not fill.

With Emily well, Joshua rode the mare to a grove of Alders a hundred yards
from the front gate of the Carlisle Estate. He tied Emily to one of the trees and
crept through the waist-deep grass to within a hundred feet of the line of cot-
tages. He whistled for Rebecca—making it sound as much like a Meadow Lark
as he could.

It took only minutes for Rebecca to run from her family's cottage, across
the lawn, and across the roadway to where he knelt in the grass. "What are you
doing here, Joshua?"

"It's been two weeks since you haven't come to see me. What happened?"

"It's my mother. She has been ill, and we think it may be consumption. I
couldn't leave her."

"Is she dying?"

"She's had this disease two other times this year." She gave a wince. "I'm
very worried about her."

Joshua looked back at Emily. "Do you think the medicine that cured Emily
would help your mother?"

"We already tried." Rebecca gave him a shrug. "It works on horses, but
she's no better."

"When will you come visit me again? I've memorized ten more Bible verses."

Rebecca smiled at Joshua and gave him a long kiss. "I love you, Joshua."

"That's one."

"What?"

74

"One kiss for each Bible verse. That was our agreement."

"I said I love you. That means that I'll kiss you whenever you want, whether you learn the verses or not." She wrapped her arms around him and gave him another long kiss.

"So, when will you come back to our garden?"

Rebecca gave a huff and looked across the field at her parents' small home. "Until my mother improves, it's better for you to come here."

"Is there a best time of day—a time when you will be free?"

"Come tomorrow in the late afternoon—around four o'clock."

Joshua smiled. "I'll be here."

Joshua was there right on time, and Rebecca met him among the trees beyond the gate.

She carried a large basket. "Look! I have a picnic for us."

"Is your mother any better?"

"Not really." She took his hand and pulled him away from the roadway to where Emily grazed on the fresh grass. She looked back at the mansion and set her burdens on the ground. "I've missed you, Joshua. I wish we could go away from all of this." She pushed back and gave him a studied look. "Do you love me?"

"I never thought I could love anybody."

"Is that a yes, or no?" She gave him a poke in the chest. "The words aren't that hard to say."

"You've changed my life, Becky."

"Tell me how, Joshua. How have I changed your life?"

"When you found me in your garden that first day—that Sunday we met—I imagined myself becoming a highwayman, or a vagabond—stealing my way across England to Scotland."

"Scotland?" She wriggled up her nose. "Why Scotland?"

"I was told by the woman who raised me that my real mother was from there." He looked to where he imagined Scotland to be. "The rolling green hills, the castles, and the rock walls that stretch across the orchards and pastures. I long for a place where everyone is friendly and kind."

"But that's the same with England, Ireland, and that describes most everywhere in Europe when there isn't a war."

He gave her a nod. "Well, someday, I'll get to Scotland and maybe I'll be able to find the relatives Emily Smoot told me I have."

"Would you take me with you when you go?"

He gave her another kiss. "If I can get myself out of this trouble, then yes, I'll take you with me." He turned and reached out for the basket. "I ran out of the bread you brought with Emily's medicine. Did you bring any more?"

"I have a dozen fresh scones, and they're all for you."

"A dozen?" He unlatched the hasp and opened the basket. There was a bottle of red wine, a meat pie, scones, and a cloth spread. "You must be the cook's best friend."

She gave him a proud grin. "I'm his best helper. He has taught me how to tell fresh things from old things—fish, fowl, vegetables, and everything else. He takes me to the village every time he buys supplies because he claims there's none like me for haggling at the markets."

"Did he ask you who was going to eat all this?"

"He knows about you and what happened to make you run away."

"Uh…"

"I did not tell him where you came from or who the master was. He only knows the circumstances, and even if he did know it was Wakehurst Place, he would never tell anybody about you."

"Does he know about John Flint—that I'm his bastard?"

"No, but everybody knows about that pirate."

"Oh?"

"Mothers and fathers tell their children bedtime stories, and their favorite stories are about John Flint."

"After seeing what real pirates do, that surprises me."

"Why?"

"I crossed the Atlantic Ocean on John Flint's ship when I was eight years old. I watched while his savage crew killed innocent husbands so they could rape their wives and daughters before throwing them alive into the sea." He shook his head. "There is nothing in piracy that children should want to hear."

"But I always thought that it must be fun being a pirate."

"It's mostly cruelty, blood, and suffering." He shook his head. "Not a life for any person with a soul." Joshua picked up the bundle next to the picnic basket and gave it a shake. "What's in this?"

"Some other things you'll need in the cave."

"Oh?" He felt at several hard points. "Like what?"

"Well, you can be sure it's not another lamb."

"I told you it was a misunderstanding." He felt another of the items in the bag.

She reached down and pulled it away. "Not yet. I want it to be a surprise."

"You're full of surprises." He helped her up onto Emily's back, pulled himself up behind her, and wrapped his free arm around her chest. As the mare began to walk, he gave her breast a gentle squeeze.

"Stop that!" She pushed his hand down to her waist. "Do that again and I'll hurt you like you've never been hurt before."

Joshua gave her a tickle and kicked Emily in the withers.

☠ ☠ ☠

It was late afternoon when they arrived at the canyon. Joshua was curious about the contents of the bundle that Becky hugged to her chest.

"It's just things." She threw her leg over Emily's neck and slipped to the ground. "Things to make your life in my garden a little nicer."

He dropped next to her, took the bag from her hand, and ran ahead. He tried to untie the knot but it would not give. He called back to her. "What kind of a knot is this?"

"It's a special they use at the grist mill to tie the bags of flour so they can't be untied. It's called a constrictor knot."

"Well, it certainly works." He pulled his knife, cut the knot, reached inside, and held up a stack of crocheted rounds. "Doilies?"

"Don't fuss!" She grabbed them from him. "There are other things in there too."

He searched the bag. "Did you get the whet stone for my knife?"

"Yes, and the hand ax and Ferrier's nails so you can build some furniture."

He held up the ax. "This is wonderful." He ran a finger across the blade. "Who gave you these things?"

"The cook—the one person other than my parents that I can trust."

"Well, by John Flint's black heart, I owe your cook for this good life he's provided me."

"Why do you always say that—by John Flint's black heart?"

"Because he does have a black heart, and I believe he eats people's hearts like everybody says."

"Did you see him do it?"

"No, but all the pirates told me that they saw him do it."

"But you didn't actually see him do it, right?"

"What does it matter? I just say that sometimes."

"Well, I wish you'd say something else."

"Like what?"

"I don't know." She gave a shrug. "Something nicer like Bless Me or Land's Sake."

Joshua pulled the oil cloth from the whet stone and pulled the ax blade across it several times. "What if I say something the pirates would say, like *bend me to a yard*?"

"What does that mean?"

"Ha!" He sighted down the blade's cutting edge at her. "I'll just stick to my father's cannibalism."

Becky gathered up the spilled items and carried them into the cave. She stood for a long moment, surveying how he had laid his things out.

He stepped next to her and looked about. "What's the matter?"

"This isn't how I would have done it."

"Well, it works for me, and you're not living here, so leave my things where they are."

She pointed. "Your bed should be over there, further from the water."

Joshua opened the basket and pulled out the wine and the glasses. "I'm hungry. Can we eat?"

"Not until everything's laid out properly."

He gave a groan and pulled the cork from the bottle.

She grabbed the bottle and held it away from him. "Please show a little patience, Joshua."

"I just wanted to taste it."

"I worked too hard making this right. I'll not abide you tasting your way through everything before I've laid it out the way I planned."

"I would like to hurry so we can get going."

She stopped laying out the napkins. "Where are we going?"

"I want to take you back to Wakehurst Place to meet my friends, John and Ned."

"Are you daft? You can't go back there with those two warrants for your head!"

"There's a grove of Cottonwood trees a furlong from the castle where I'll leave you and Emily while I go ahead to see if the coast is clear. It will be dark when we get there, and if it's safe to go closer, I'll wave for you to come." He picked up one of the yellow napkins and waved it over his head. "I'll wave this from the stable rooftop to let you know the coast is clear."

"I believe you about John and Ned, that they're wonderful friends, but I don't need to meet them for you to prove their friendship."

"But you have to meet them. They have to know that I'm well, and I want them to know how special you are to me."

She shook her head slowly from side to side in pity and disgust. "Your stubborn spirit got you in this trouble in the first place. I won't allow it to take you from me."

"Take me from you?"

"What if Lord Lyddell sees you?"

"He won't."

"Every choice we make comes with consequences—some good and some bad. This thing you want to do for me could get you killed."

"I'll be careful, Becky."

"Is it so important that you tell your friends about me that you'd risk your life for it?"

"Besides, I need to tell them that Emily is well."

"They don't need to know that either."

"But I want them to know, so make up your mind." He pushed the folded napkin into his pocket. "Go with me or I'll go by myself."

She gave him a long look and shook her head. "I like you, Joshua, but I also value my life and my freedom. What you are doing could jeopardize both of us."

He ground his teeth. "Does that mean you will or won't go with me?"

"Sorry. You'll have to go alone."

☠ ☠ ☠

Joshua reached Wakehurst Place just after ten o'clock. The old castle stood on a man-made mound that was thirty feet above the surrounding land. This came in very handy when an enemy tried to attack through the ground fog— exactly the situation as Joshua tied Emily to a Cottonwood tree. He climbed up the hill and watched the castle for several minutes. Finally, convinced that nobody was on guard, he ran up and across the paddocks, through the garden, and up to the back of John and Ned's cottage.

As usual, none of the windows or doors were locked. He pushed open the window at the rear—away from the mansion—and looked inside. There was a fire in the metal stove, and the smell of stew filled the rock building.

Joshua called in a loud whisper. "Ned!"

"What?" Ned sat up from his bed and looked toward the voice. "Who's there?"

"Over here." Joshua pushed the window open and waved his hand.

"Are you daft, Joshua? There are two King's warrants for your head."

Joshua climbed through the window, jumped down, and brushed himself off. "Where's John?"

Ned pointed out across the courtyard. "He was getting ready to lie down when he remembered we were out of coffee. He went across to the kitchen to fill the tin."

"Go get him."

Ned hesitated. "It's been months. We were sure you were gone back to Savannah."

"I'll explain when you two return."

Ned turned, ran across the cobblestones, and disappeared into the kitchen. Joshua walked around the small cottage savoring the familiar room and its smells. *Maybe I was stupid...all for a name...I do miss all of this!* He heard footsteps coming across the courtyard, so he ducked behind the wardrobe.

John stepped inside and whispered. "Laddy?"

Joshua stepped out and spread his arms." Aye! In the flesh!"

"What are you doing here?"

"You're not glad to see me?"

"Of course, I'm glad to see you, but you've taken such a risk coming here like this."

"I just wanted to tell you I found the canyon and that Emily is cured."

"Cured?" Ned stepped close. "How?"

"I met a girl named Rebecca Keyes. She lives at the Carlisle estate. She had the medicine Emily needed."

"That's all good, Laddy, and I'm right pleased for you, but there's two King's warrants for your head. If Lord Lyddell catches you here, he'll have you shot and the two of us will be thrown in irons for harboring you."

Joshua looked to Ned and back to John. "That morning I left...what happened?"

"By the time Graves came out to see what the noise was—the broken wall—you were gone and there were a dozen others already gathered about to see the mess. Ned and I pretended the commotion woke us."

"Then Graves—"

"If anybody sees you here, they'll have all the proof they need that we helped you escape." John pointed back the way Joshua had come. "Quick, Laddy. You have to—"

Before John could finish, the cottage door was kicked inward and slammed back against the wall. Silhouetted against the light from the mansion stood Charles Lyddell and Graves—each man holding two duelling pistols.

"So, it was you!" Lyddell pointed both of his pistols at Joshua's heart.

Instinctively, Joshua dove down and to the right, and then scrambled away toward the window. Lyddell's first pistol discharged, tearing across the left side of his face. Graves stood to Lyddell's right, directly in line with John. Both the butler's pistols fired at the fleeing youth, but before Charles could raise his second pistol to take aim, Joshua had leaped out through the window. In a moment, he was across the paddocks, down the moors, and back into the evening ground fog where he had left Emily.

"You were correct, sir." Graves stepped to John and kicked him in the hip. "Get up, old man! You're on your way to the gallows!"

"He can't!" Ned knelt next to his mentor. "Look!" Ned pulled back John's jacket to reveal his blood-soaked shirt. The ball from one of the pistols had pierced John's chest just below his heart. The old man was senseless, and with every breath, bright red blood bubbled from his mouth and ran down his cheek onto the floor. Ned looked up at Graves. "You devil! You've killed him!"

During moments of rage and desperation, a man will do things that he will later regret. Joshua's attack on his cruel master was such a moment, and now Ned's fury rose against Graves for the death of the only father he had known. The attack was predictable, and Ned was dispatched with a ball from Lord Lyddell's second fowling pistol. The boy fell next to his dying mentor.

Graves stepped to John's body and nudged him with the point of his shoe. "It was my pistol that downed the old man. I was aiming at Thomas."

"And it was mine that killed Ned." Charles walked to the window and touched a smear of blood on the sill. "Thomas is injured." In a moment, the two were outside and around the cottage where a trail of blood shared the soil with Joshua's foot prints. "Call out the dogs." Charles looked out at the edge of the fog bank. "If his wound is mortal, it will be a short hunt."

"What about these two in the cottage?

Lyddell turned and looked at the two bodies. "We'll notify the constable but not until I've displayed their bodies in the morning for all our servants to see."

CHAPTER TEN:

The Seamstress' Thread

All Joshua's instincts were screaming for escape and survival. The mad dash across the paddocks and down the hill to the waiting fog seemed to take an eternity. By the time he reached Emily, blood had soaked the left side of his jacket. To his surprise, there was very little pain from the wound, only the strange vacant chill to his teeth and left cheek.

He stopped running twenty feet from Emily and put a hand to his face. "Aaah!"

It was the sound a wounded animal would make. The bullet had laid open his left cheek from ear to mouth. The flap of skin hung from his jaw, exposing his teeth. He stumbled for a moment in shock, and then managed to climb up onto Emily's back. He rode for over an hour before he felt safe to stop and see to his wound. *Becky's napkin*! After several failed attempts to close the wound and tie the napkin in place, Joshua laid down on his right side so that the flap of skin would cooperate. Exhausted and in shock, Joshua fell into a fitful sleep.

The eastern sky was just beginning to pink when Joshua arrived at the Carlisle estate. A servant, who was beating rugs near the kitchen door, saw Joshua first and ran to him. She put her hands to her face in shock. "You're Joshua, aren't you?" She looked up at the napkin tied about his head. "Oh, my God! What happened to your face?"

Joshua just looked at her, wondering how much Becky had told the servants about him. He slumped from Emily's back, stumbled for a moment, and stood against the mare for support.

"Hold still while I..." She untied the knot and tried to undo the cloth from his face, but the blood had dried, making its removal impossible. She twisted up her own face at the possible damage to the hidden flesh. "Can you talk?"

"I on'd ow." Joshua tried to mouth the words, but they came out too garbled to understand. He shook his head and pointed to the mansion.

"I'm Katy—Becky's friend!" She turned toward the house but stopped and looked back at Joshua. "You need to be stitched up!"

"Behee!" Joshua mumbled the word and grabbing at the girl. "Gea Behee!"

"Yes! Of course! You want Becky!" She pointed at the kitchen. "She's...oh, my God!"

"Ge har!" He looked about for Rebecca. "Pees! Ge har!"

"I can't get her right now!" Katy pointed. "She's in town with the cook, shopping! It could be another hour before they return!" She grabbed his arm, pulled him across the road, around the back of the mansion, and into the kitchen. She pushed him across to a bench near the stove. "Wait here! Don't move! I'll get help!"

Joshua nodded while the girl rushed off. A moment later, two other maids and a lad of twelve ran into the kitchen. The boy looked at Joshua and ran out. A moment later, Katy returned with a stack of fresh hand towels, followed by an older woman carrying a carpet bag with sewing needles piercing its upper edge.

"So, you're Becky's secret friend?" The woman's tone was motherly and kind. She was in her early forties, of slight build, and reminded Joshua of Emily Smoot. He stood and took a step toward her. "I'm Misses Steiner—Lady Carlisle's personal assistant." She held up the sewing bag. "I'm also the household seamstress."

Joshua put a hand to his injured cheek and the untied napkin that was hanging from his face. "Ahh…"

"Don't try to talk, Joshua. It will only hurt you." She gave the napkin a gentle pull. "I need to take a look at your face, but it won't come loose until the blood releases the napkin."

She set a folded blanket on the table and gave it a pat. "Get up here, Joshua." She helped him onto the table and turned him onto his right side so she could tend to the wound. "I love Old Testament names, especially yours. Did you know that Jesus is the same name?"

He turned his head slightly and looked up at her. Katy set a kettle on the stove and added several pieces of wood to the fire.

"I know you can't speak right now, but it will be much better once I sew your face back together."

Tears began to well in Joshua's eyes. He wanted to reach out and take hold of this kind and gentle woman but restrained himself.

Katy touched Misses Steiner's arm. "The tea water is only warm. It'll take a few minutes to boil."

She pushed a bowl to Katy. "Pour some of the warm water into this, swish it about, and refill it. We'll have to remove this napkin and the caked blood from the lad's face before we can see the damage."

A moment later, the napkin was soaked with water, causing the blood to release the napkin. As it did, Misses Steiner began to hum a hymn that Emily Smoot had sung years before. Joshua looked up and tried to talk.

"No, no, Joshua." She stroked his forehead. "Don't try to talk yet."

He reached out and grabbed her hand. Tears cascaded across his face.

"You know that hymn, don't you?"

He nodded.

"Your mother?"

He nodded again as more tears streamed across his face.

She applied more warm water to the napkin and peeled back another section. "That was the first hymn I ever sang after I told the Lord I believed in Him."

"Mmmm!" Joshua closed his eyes and sobbed quietly.

She stopped pulling the napkin for a moment. "I'm sorry. I'm trying too hard, aren't I?" He closed his eyes, so she continued humming. She finished the hymn at the same moment the napkin finally let go. "There we are! Now we'll swab all the remaining blood from your cheek and see about stitching you back together." She turned to her sewing bag, pulled out two needles, and a fresh ball of tatting string. She wrapped one of the needles in cloth and bent it to form the letter C. "Here, Katy. This needle and the string need boiling."

A short time later, Joshua's face was cleaned and ready. Misses Steiner threaded the needle and began humming the same hymn quietly. Joshua gave her a pained look and a groan as she pulled the two inside edges of his flesh together and inserted the needle. "I'll have to sew the inside together first, and then do it all over again on the outside. There's nothing I can do about the pain." She took another stitch and began to hum again. "On the inside, it will be a row of separate knots. In two weeks, I expect the flesh will have grown back together enough that you can remove the knots yourself."

The hall boy burst into the kitchen. "She's here! Becky and the cook are just now rolling around the building from town!" He turned and ran from the kitchen and could be heard calling to Rebecca. Joshua tried to sit up.

Misses Steiner pushed him down. "Patience, young man. Becky will be at your side soon enough."

There was a flurry of excited voices, opening and closing of doors, and running feet.

"Joshua!" Rebecca ran to his side and took his hand. "Oh, my God! Look at you!" He blinked and nodded.

Misses Steiner pushed his head down onto the towel. "Hold still!" She took another stitch and pulled the thread through his flesh.

Rebecca touched the seamstress' arm. "Is that a sword or a gunshot wound?"

Joshua held up a hand and made a motion like the firing lock dropping on a pistol.

"Oh, Joshua. I warned you that something like this might happen."

Misses Steiner looked up at Rebecca. "He already knows that, child. This is a time for healing, not for scolding."

Rebecca gripped Joshua's hands. "What about your friends? Did Lord Lyddell discover that it was them who helped you escape?"

"Patience, Rebecca. He'll be able to talk a little after I'm finished."

For the next hour, there was much weeping and an equal amount of prayer.

Finally, Misses Steiner cut the thread and sat back. "That's all I can do for you, Joshua. You'll have a scar from your ear to the corner of your mouth for the rest of your life, and I'm afraid that even a beard won't hide it."

"Thank you." Joshua winced at the pain and turned to Rebecca and nodded. "You were right about my going back."

"What about John and Ned? Were they hurt too?"

"I don't know." He sucked air through his teeth and kept his jaw closed as he continued. "If they lived through this, they'll go to the gallows for sure."

Rebecca shook her head slowly and took him into her arms. She looked at Misses Steiner. "Can he stay here for a while?"

The older woman shook her head. "Only for a moment. We would all be in trouble if Lord Carlisle found out that we've helped a wanted man." She gathered up her things and replaced them in her sewing bag. "Say your goodbyes and then Joshua must be on his way."

Rebecca escorted Joshua to the courtyard where one of the stable boys was holding Emily. "Don't go yet. If you do, I won't be able to see you until next Sunday." She looked up into his eyes. "You know that I still love you."

"My mother loved me, and she was killed for it. John and Ned loved me, and I fear that they have also been killed."

"Nobody is going to kill me for loving you, Joshua."

"How can I know that? How can I know that you will be safe?"

"It's in your heart, Joshua." She put her hand on his chest. "It hurts me when we're apart. It must hurt you too."

"Yes—almost more than I can bare."

"Well?" She waited. "What do you think that is? What do you think that yearning to be together is if it isn't love?"

He looked away toward Emily.

"Can't you say it? Can't you tell me that you love me too?"

"After how stupid I've been?" Joshua reached up and touched his cheek. "I've decided that I'm not worthy of your love, Becky."

"Hogwash! I'm the one in charge of who I choose to love, and I've chosen you!"

"After all this—the stupid things I keep doing—you can still say that?"

"You don't understand love, do you?"

He shook his head. "It only brings pain and death."

"You poor, pathetic thing." She backed away another step. "Perhaps you should leave right now, and all this week, think about me. Think about what I mean to you." She took several frustrated breaths. "Then, next Sunday while everybody is at church, I'll come to the garden early and we'll make some decisions, okay?" She stepped up to him, pulled him down, and leaned close to kiss him. As he pursed his lips, he let out a moan. "Yes—it hurts to kiss." She kissed his cheek. "Now go and search your heart to see if I'm still there."

☠ ☠ ☠

Joshua and Emily arrived back at the garden with Rebecca's words echoed about in his mind. He was hungry, but his mouth was too painful for anything but water. Sleeping was difficult with the memory of what he had done to hurt Rebecca and his close friends.

He got up the next morning, stepped out into the open, and looked up at the clear sky. "I want to love you, Becky, but I know it will only hurt you."

He looked about the sky at the passing clouds. "God, I believed in you when I was small—in Savannah with my mother—but I don't know anymore. I watch people go to church. They dress up and smile at each other, but then they treat their fellow pew-sitters no better than the heathens." He waited, as if God would say something. "I love Becky! You know that! I want to tell you, but I'm afraid it will be just like all the others! My love will only cause you pain!"

The next Sunday morning, Joshua was up early, waited, and watched the lake shore where Rebecca always walked to her secret garden. His face still hurt, especially when he ate or drank the water from his spring.

He waited all day, and she never came. When the sun was nearing the horizon, he leaped onto Emily and rode to the Carlisle Mansion. The stable master was the first to see him.

"You there!" The man walked out to the field. "Are you Joshua Smoot?" Joshua reined the horse back several paces as the man approached and took hold of Emily's bridle. "If you're looking for Becky Keyes, she's gone!"

"Gone?"

"They're all gone."

"What are you saying?" Joshua looked around the estate. "Who's gone?"

"All the domestics and their families were ordered off the land Tuesday last. The Gypsies took advantage of the order by taking most of their money for transportation north to London. They left Wednesday about noon."

"Why?" Joshua reached up and touched his cheek. "Was it because of me?"

"No. They weren't needed any more."

"But the land? The gardens?"

"It's been coming for months. The land has been turned over to the sheep, and it only takes one shepherd for each flock. The cook and some of the down-stairs staff will remain to tend the family garden."

"She must have told you that I would come looking for her."

The man pulled a piece of parchment from his pocket. "Yes, and she wrote you a letter."

Joshua tore the wax seal away and read quickly.

My dearest Joshua:

Please forgive me for leaving like this, but I had no choice. We were told just yesterday afternoon that we were being put off the land for the sheep. I wanted to come to you, but with everything that had to be done, there was no time. All this was too much for my mother. She has had a relapse and I simply can't leave her side.

Father tells me that we are going to the small port town of Lambeth first. He has a friend there who should take us in. Father says that if that does not work out, then we will move down the Thames River, from town to town until he finds work.

I told you that I loved you, Joshua, but you couldn't, or wouldn't repeat the words. I am hoping and praying that you came to the mansion, and that you are reading this letter. I am also praying that you have found the love that I know is inside you, and that you will follow me.

All my love,

Becky

CHAPTER ELEVEN:
Trouble at Lambeth

Joshua didn't remember the ride back to the lake. His mind raced, fearing that he would never see Rebecca again, and angry that the families had been thrown off the land. At the garden, he gathered up only the essentials. His longbow and arrows, all the dried meat, his water bag, and several other items. All he had for directions was Rebecca's letter and the road that left Weir Wood north toward London. The roadway became littered with people sitting next to camp fires. He searched for Rebecca, but she was not there. In desperation, he reached the Thames River and the port town of Lambeth on the third day.

"The docks." Joshua scanned the letter for any clue where she and her parents might be. He folded the letter, replaced it in his pocket, and set out again. "Where are you, Becky?"

The docks at Lambeth were a confusing tangle of bowsprits and rigging, and a collection of the dispossessed families removed from the land and left with no hope for a future. Joshua dismounted from Emily and walked through the press of humanity.

A man with black skin that looked like leather stepped in front of Joshua with his bony hand out. "Have you anything to eat, kind sir?"

Joshua put his hand to his food bag.

"No!" A man in a dark coat grabbed Joshua's hand. "If you have any food, don't waste it on him."

"But he's a man like you and me."

"He's diseased and will die soon."

Joshua pulled loose from the man and stepped back to the Negro. "I have a little dried meat." He pulled the remainder of his food from the bag at his waist. "Here, you can have half of what I have."

The Negro took the meat and began to cry. "God will bless you for this."

The other man gave Joshua a push. "You're a fool!" He turned and was gone.

Joshua continued his search, stopping every twenty yards to make sure he had not missed Rebecca. He grabbed a man in his thirties who was passing with a small chest in his arms. "There's a girl! She's fifteen years old! Her name is Rebecca Keyes!"

"Fifteen, huh?" The man twisted away, spat on Joshua, and pointed toward the line of inns beyond the docks. "I'd look to the brothels for the girl, and while you're inside, we'll kill and eat your horse."

In a flash, Joshua threw the man down and pinned him to the boards with his knife at the scrawny throat. "It'll be your heart they'll be eating!"

"Murderer!" The man cried out like a child. "He's gonna cut out my heart and eat it!"

Joshua jumped up and grabbed Emily's bridle. He gave the man a vicious kick to the leg and pointed the knife at his face. "If I see you again, by John Flint's black heart, I *will* slit your throat!" The man scrambled away.

By late afternoon, Joshua had walked Dock Street from end to end four times. In despair, he turned Emily about to the south to escape this hell hole of England. While he set himself to leap up onto her back, he felt a tug at the bag of dried meat at his waist. He whirled around. It was the same man, and now he had cut away the last of Joshua's food.

"You!" Joshua grabbed the thief by the hand, twisted the bag loose, and bent his index finger backward until it snapped in half at the knuckle. While the thief screamed, Joshua grabbed his other hand and broke the other index finger the same way.

"First you insult me and threaten to kill my horse, and now you steal my food!" He pointed at the man's hands. "Twice you've accosted me, and twice you've been punished!" He gave him a kick that sent him sprawling across the worn boards.

Joshua leaped onto Emily's back, turned her about toward the south, and started picking his way through the crowd of refugees.

He had traveled no more than a hundred feet when somebody called out to him. "You, there, on the horse!" It was a soldier. "Stop in the name of the King!" Joshua looked about at the people and his various ways of escape. He put down his head in despair.

"That's him!" The man with the broken fingers pointing at Joshua' face. "See? I told you that he had that cut on his face!"

Joshua slid to the ground and gave the man a defiant stare.

"This will cost you!" The soldier pushed him with the butt of his rifle. "I might even get to flog you myself!"

"My horse!"

"I'll hold her for him." As the thief spoke the lie, his hand went to his knife. "When you're done flogging him, I'll be right here."

The moment Joshua and the soldier were gone, the man carefully wrapped one of the bridle thongs around his wrist and pulled Emily into a side street. "Your flesh is gonna make a bunch of hungry people very happy tonight and make me a rich man at the same time."

☠ ☠ ☠

Rebecca Keyes had lost both her parents in a matter of days. While nearing the port town of Lambeth, the Gypsies stopped and ordered Rebecca and her parents from the wagon with their meager belongings.

"We paid you to take us to Lambeth. What are you doing?"

"This stand of trees is at the edge of Lambeth. We have done what you paid us to do."

"How much further is it to the river?"

"You and those two can carry your things there in an hour." With that, the Gypsy turned his rig about and rode away.

"What are we going to do, father?"

He looked around at the other refugees. "I…" He knelt next to his wife. "The man said it was an hour walk, Peggy. Do you think you can do that if we help you?"

His wife gave a cough and pushed herself up. "I believe I can if you and Rebecca can carry our things."

"Sure." James looked to his daughter. "We can do that, can't we?"

"Of course, we can, father." She looked to the west. "But it will be dark shortly. Shouldn't we find a place near one of the fires and rest for the night?"

"Probably best." As he bent to pick up one of the bundles, a man called from a wagon.

"You three, there! Do you need a ride to Lambeth?"

James stood and turned. "Yes—we do!"

"Well, I have room on my wagon for you and your goods." He stopped next to them. "Throw them on and we'll be on our way."

As James set the last of the four bundles atop the wagon, he turned to watch Rebecca help her mother to her feet. "Forgive us for being so slow, but my wife has been ill, and—" Before James could finish, the driver laid his whip to the horse and started away.

"Hey!" James leaped onto the back of the wagon and stepped quickly through the bags and boxes toward the driver. "What are you doing?"

As he reached out for the driver, the man turned and fired his pistol at James' chest.

Rebecca screamed as she and her mother watched him stumble backward and off the wagon. He hit the ground, rolled once, and lay still. "Father!" Rebecca ran to him, but the lead ball had accomplished its grisly work.

While the wagon and their belongings rolled away, Peggy stumbled to the two. "Is he…?"

"He shot him, Mother! He took our things and then he shot him!"

Peggy let out a scream and fell onto James' body. "What are we going to do, Becky? We have nothing, and we don't know how to find his friend."

The three lay in the roadway until the next wagon came. "In the roadway! Move out of our way so we can pass!"

Rebecca looked up at the man and his wife. "He's dead. A man stole our things and shot my father!"

"That's none of our concern." He pointed. "Pull him off the road so we can pass."

Two days without food, water, or protection from the harsh elements quickly robbed Peggy of her strength. Rebecca had nothing to dig their graves, and like so many others, eventually had to abandon her parents' bodies at the roadside.

She arrived in the port town of Lambeth the next day and joined the displaced throngs. "Please, Lord. Help me. Don't abandon me too."

There was no work, and every time a local church group offered their charity to the needy, the thieves snatched up everything and sold it elsewhere at a profit. Rebecca wandered the streets of Lambeth the rest of the day asking every merchant for work. With the constant inflow of people from the south, there were no jobs to be had.

Frustrated and hungry, Rebecca stopped at the intersection of Great Surrey and Stanford streets and turned about in the hope that somebody might stop and help her. "Nobody cares, Lord. Please help me!"

"Pardon me, Lassy." It was a man with a wooden box with several bowls of food. "I heard you praying."

"I'm alone and have nothing." She smelled the food. "I…"

"If you need to pray, you should do it down there at Christ Church instead of in the middle of the street." He pointed south. "And if you're hungry, they're giving out soup and bread."

"I am—hungry." She looked to where dozens of people were gathering. "Thank you."

"You'd best hurry, Lassy. There's a lot of hungry people so the food won't last very long."

Rebecca took her bowl of soup and bread to one of the pews, thanked the Lord, and began to eat.

"You're one of them, aren't you?"

She looked up at the elderly woman. "I'm…"

"I could tell from your clothes. You're from one of the estates down toward Brighton."

"Yes—the Carlisle Estate. My parents and I were put off the land a few days ago because of the sheep."

"With your parents?" She looked around. "Are they here?"

"No, they both…"

"What happened?" The woman sat down next to Rebecca.

"A thief stole our belongings, and when my father tried to stop him, the man shot him."

"And your mother?"

"She was sick with consumption, and…" With tears running down her cheeks, she looked at the woman. "I'm alone now and I don't know what to do."

"You're like so many young girls I've spoken to these last few weeks since this happened."

"And what did you tell them? What are they doing now?"

"It hurts me to tell you this, but unless you have family who will take you in, you are left with the same two choices as those other girls."

"What two choices?"

"For those unwilling to indenture themselves and travel to the colonies, all they have left is prostitution, and that is an ungodly life."

"Then tell me about that other thing--indenturing myself to the colonies."

☠ ☠ ☠

Two hours later, with her indenture contract in hand, Rebecca stepped aboard the schooner *Maiden*. She was met by a young man wearing some sort of naval uniform.

"Yes, this is the right ship, but we will not cast off for another hour—not until we get the final count and everybody is aboard." He nodded toward the docks. "I'm Edwin Drake, the captain's son and his first officer. If you have any family here, this will be your last chance to tell them farewell."

"Uh…" She looked back toward the church. "Yes—I'll do that. Thank you."

On her way back to Christ Church to see whether they had any donated clothing, she spotted the brood mare, Emily, being led from Dock Street into an alley by a man with injured hands.

Rebecca ran to the man and grabbed the reigns. "Where did you get that horse?"

"If you're wanting to eat a piece of her, you'll have to pay me in coin or script like everybody else."

Rebecca looked down at his deformed fingers. "He did that to you, didn't he?"

"Who are you talking about?"

"A young man with a cut on his face." She pulled her finger down across her cheek.

"Aye, and he had an old scar on his right hand too."

"Where is he?"

"Pay me or I won't tell you."

She grabbed one of the broken fingers and gave it a twist. "I asked you a question!"

"Ah!' The man dropped to his knees in agony. "He's on Dock Street just past the ships! The soldier is taking him west to the constable's house!"

She gave the finger another twist and pulled the reigns loose. Just as Joshua had taught her, she swung her body up and onto Emily's bare back, turned the mare about, and rode back through the alley to the docks.

"Out of my way!" Rebecca urged the horse forward through the sea of displaced people. Only those who would be stepped on by Emily's hoofs paid heed to her warnings. She kicked Emily in the withers, setting the large horse into a trot. Now, the sound of her hoofs on the dock boards caught the attention of the throngs, causing them to scatter.

Rebecca spotted the soldier. Just as the thief had said, Joshua was walking ahead of him at gunpoint. Rebecca looked about and noticed that there was a parallel street just fifty feet to the south. She slowed Emily to a walk and turned her into the nearest alley. Once on the smaller street, she turned the mare to the right and urged her into a trot, watching for Joshua and the soldier at each alleyway.

When she was confident that she had outdistanced them, she turned through another alley back to Dock Street, and urged Emily into a gallop. Emerging from the alley, she began screaming. "Help me!" She dropped the reigns and kicked the mare in the withers. "She's gone crazy and I can't stop her! Help me!"

Joshua recognized Rebecca and Emily and knew instantly what she was up to. The soldier, however, was not sure what he should do.

"You're one of the King's men! Do your duty and save that lass!"

The soldier raised his rifle in both hands and stepped forward several paces, but Emily kept coming at a full gallop. While the soldier's attention was distracted, Joshua slipped into an alleyway, ran through to the next street, and hid among a stand of wagons.

Passing the confused soldier, Rebecca reached down, grabbed the reigns, and turned the mare toward Joshua's hiding place.

"Becky! Over here!"

She jumped down from the horse and rushed to his waiting arms. For the next several minutes, they held onto each other as if they would die if they let go. After a flurry of kisses, Rebecca looked down the crowded street. "We can't stay here! That soldier will be looking for you."

"I got your note." Joshua leaped up onto Emily and reached down for Rebecca. "Where are your parents?"

"Not now!" She took his hand and swung up behind him. Once settled, the two galloped through the streets and then turned south onto the highway. When finally clear of the town and the press of people, Joshua stopped Emily and the two slid off her back to the ground. Rebecca grabbed his face to kiss him.

"Ouch!"

"Oh, I'm sorry!" She inspected the stitches. "It's only been eight or nine days."

"I didn't think I'd ever find you."

"I didn't think you'd come looking."

"Where are your parents?"

She pointed south and wiped the tears from her eyes. "They're gone."

"I don't understand. Weren't they with you?"

She closed her eyes at the thought of what happened. "My father was shot by a thief several days ago. He took everything we had."

"What about your mother? Where is she?"

She touched her heart. "Father died quickly. It was cold and wet and Mother refused to leave his body. The Lord knows that I tried to get her away from there, but she died of consumption right there, next to my father's body. It only took a day and a night." She began to sob. "I didn't have anything for digging a grave and nobody would stop to help me."

"Why Lambeth? What was there for you?"

"My father told us that he had a friend who would take us in until father could find work."

"Did you find him?"

"I went to the house, but he wasn't there. Three families had moved in and none of them knew where he had gone."

Joshua looked back along the road. "There were farms along the road. I can borrow a shovel."

"There isn't time."

"Why not? What's—"

"My ship departs for America this afternoon with the tide." She pulled a folded piece of parchment from her apron pocket and handed it to him. "With my parents gone and no prospects for work, I have indentured myself to a family in Charles Town, South Carolina."

"You'll be a slave." Joshua took the document and read it quickly. "Seven years?"

"It was this or prostitution."

"Wait!" He held up the contract. "How can this be better than what we had at our canyon?"

"Without my parents or you, what did I have?"

"But you still have me, Rebecca."

"No, I don't." She backed away a step and shook her head. "You tried to kill Lord Lyddell. You have two King's warrants against you."

"We have each other. We have Emily." He pointed south. "We could ride back to your garden! I can feed us!"

"And how long can we live like that?"

"We'd be alive." Joshua gritted his teeth and looked about the roadway. It was choked with the other refugees marching toward Lambeth. "Alright. Tell me about being indentured."

"It's a trade—my passage to America in exchange for seven years servitude to whoever sponsors me. I am told that I will be provided with everything I need, and possibly a small wage so that I can buy personal items."

"What happens when your seven years are finished?"

"I'll be a free person, and by then I will have learned enough skills and become friends with enough people in the town to be able to get good employment."

"These people in Charles Town—could they use a stable hand?"

"I don't know—just that they will pay for my crossing passage, and I will repay my debt with seven years of service."

"If we arrived together—as man and wife—"

"You'd indenture yourself for me? You'd go to Charles Town with me?"

"With those warrants on my head and you leaving, it seems I have no other choice."

"Yes!" She looked up at the angle of the sun. "We'll have to be quick!" He lifted her back up onto Emily. "It's a small ship—the *Maiden*—but I'm certain there would be room for you!" Joshua swung himself up behind her and they rode back north toward Lambeth.

☠ ☠ ☠

The solicitor was a skinny man in his late thirties. He was dressed in black, with a high white collar that was in dire need of chalking. He looked up at the young man in line ahead of Joshua and Rebecca. "Your name?"

"Clive Stevens."

The solicitor pulled a list close and searched for a moment. "Very good— no warrants for your arrest." He took a preprinted parchment from a stack and filled in the man's name. He tore the document in half, handed the lad his half, and placed the other in an envelope. "There." He pointed at a ship at the east end of the docks. "It's the *Mulberry*. She'll depart for Richmond, Virginia with the others in an hour."

"Thank you, sir." The young man collected his things and hurried away.

The solicitor made an entry in his journal and then looked up at Rebecca. "I remember you. You already have your papers, and you should already be aboard your ship, young lady."

She reached around and pulled Joshua forward to the table. "Yes but—"

"Rebecca!" Joshua pulled her away several paces and whispered. "That paper is a list of the King's warrants. My name is on it."

"No!"

"I can't go with you."

It took her a desperate moment. "No—not as Joshua Smoot." She looked back to the solicitor as another couple stepped to his table. "But you can go as somebody else."

"I…" He thought for a moment. "John Manley! Since he was killed, he can't be on that list." He nodded at the line. "I'll go with you as John Manley."

"Wait."

"What?"

"When we decided to do this, you suggested that we could arrive in Charles Town as man and wife."

"It would make a difference, wouldn't it?"

"Yes, but before we do this, there are three words—little words but important words—that I need to hear from you."

"Yes—I know those words." He took her face in his hands and gave her a kiss. "I love you, Rebecca Keyes, with all my heart, and I know one thing about maritime law."

"Oh"

"Ships captains have the authority to perform marriages. We will be married at sea."

They stepped back in line, and as they reached the table, she took Joshua by the arm. "This is my betrothed. We need a sponsor in Charles Town who will take a husband and a wife."

"None of this is chiseled in stone, so where you are assigned to spend your seven years may be determined after you reach Charles Town." The solicitor gave Joshua a suspicious look and turned back to Rebecca. "The two of you are betrothed, yet when you were here before, you were going off to Charles Town alone."

Joshua stepped forward. "We were separated and I just found her." He gave the man a shrug. "It's a complicated story."

The man lowered his glasses and gave Joshua a long look. "Lies are usually complicated, aren't they?"

"It isn't a lie, sir."

Rebecca put a hand on Joshua's arm and gave him a forceful squeeze. "Does it really matter whether it's a complicated story? He wants to indenture himself so he can come with me to Charles Town. You make money from that, right?"

The man looked at Rebecca for a moment and then smiled. "Right!" He pulled a document close and ran his finger down to her name. "From what you told me about yourself, I put your name next to a family by the name of Abercrombie."

"Yes!" Rebecca pulled out her contract. "You said they owned a small estate near the harbor."

"This family wanted a single woman, not a married one. That's why I wrote your name there."

"John's a hard worker, and a quick learner." Rebecca turned and looked up at Joshua and back to the solicitor. She held her contract out to the man. "If he can't go with me on the *Maiden*, then I'm afraid I won't be able to go either."

The man tapped a name and address on the list. "There is another family on my list in Charles Town who is requesting a husband and wife. The husband is to tend the stables and the grounds, and the wife is to be an assistant to the cook." He looked up at Rebecca's breasts. "They would prefer a wet nurse."

"We're not married yet."

"Captain Drake could marry you the moment the *Maiden* is at sea."

Joshua nodded. "Yes—we know that."

The solicitor pulled out a fresh parchment, dipped his quill in the ink, and looked up at Joshua. "Your name?"

"My name is John Manley."

The solicitor gave Rebecca a questioning look. "I thought I heard her call you Joshua as you rode up."

"You must have heard wrong, sir. His name is John Manley."

Before he wrote the name on the parchment, he scanned quickly down the list of outstanding King's warrants. "Very well, John." A moment later, he turned the document sideways, tore it in half, and put one half on a stack next to the journal. He held up the other half. "Here. This half is yours. That other half will be delivered to Captain with the rest." He sat back and rubbed his neck. "When you reach Charles Town, Captain Drake will deliver it to a solicitor like me who will make your final assignment. On the day your obligation is fulfilled, if the two halves match, you are a free man." He pointed east along the docks. "The *Maiden* is the third one. I would suggest you two go aboard now."

"Thank you, sir." Rebecca started pulling Joshua away but he resisted. "What's the matter?"

"Emily. We can't take her to America with us."

"Well, of course we can't." Her tone was what a mother would use on a disobedient child.

"We'll need money." He turned back to the solicitor. "Do you know any-body who would want to purchase my brood mare?"

The little man looked up from his papers. "I'm a man of the law, not the stables. I wouldn't know her worth, except cut up and sold for dinner to these desperate souls around us."

"Back at—" Joshua held his tongue. "At the estate where I was employed in the stables, her common worth would be thirty pounds. But I have discovered she is carrying a foal."

"What is a foal?"

"She's pregnant, and the sire is from a champion line. That foal will be worth fifty pounds. Rebecca and I need money for when we arrive in America. Would you take her for thirty pounds?"

The man studied Joshua for a moment and then stood from his desk. With a grunt, he forced himself straight and rubbed his backside. "Let me take a look at her." He walked all the way around the mare, touched her as he went, and then patting her withers. Finally, he forced her mouth open and inspected her teeth. "She looks to be about eight years old."

"I think you know horses better than you let on, sir."

The man returned to his desk and pulled out his money box. "Yes, I'll buy your mare but for twenty-five pounds."

"Will you promise me that she will not be killed for her flesh?"

"Yes—I promise that she and her foal will live a long and happy life at my estate."

"Thank you." Joshua joined Rebecca at Emily, gave her a kiss on the muzzle, and whispered. "Goodbye, Emily. I hate to leave you like this, but I have no choice."

"John! Rebecca!" The man pointed. "Your ship is making ready to cast off. Cut your goodbye's short and get aboard."

At the *Maiden*, Joshua stopped at the gangplank, held up the two indenture documents, and called out. "Two more indentured servants to Charles Town! Permission to come aboard!"

"Aye!" The captain was of medium build and in his late fifties. He walked to the rail to meet the couple. "You must be a seafaring man."

"Pardon?"

"Everybody else who's come aboard before you has been a dirt farmer. None of them has asked permission like you did young man."

"I spent some time on a ship several years back."

"How much time?"

"I crossed the Atlantic from Savannah to Brighton. I was young, but I watched the crew handle the sails day and night for six weeks. I know the ropes, as they say."

"Well, I can always use another able-bodied seaman."

"I'm strong and I'm a quick learner, sir. I'll help whenever I can."

"I like you." He offered his hand. "I'm Captain Michael Drake."

"I'm John Manley." Joshua turned to Rebecca. "This is my betrothed, Rebecca Keyes."

"Betrothed, huh?" It was a voice calling from aft. Joshua turned as a young man in his early twenties stepped up from the companionway and stood on the deck. He looked Rebecca up and down. "Such a pretty maiden aboard the *Maiden*."

"This is my son, Edwin."

Edwin stepped forward to Rebecca, took her hand, and kissed it. "Very pleased to make your acquaintance, Rebecca Keyes."

Joshua bristled at the obvious attention Edwin was giving to Rebecca. He put his arm around her shoulders and pulled her away. He offered his hand to the captain's son. "I'm John Manley. We're hoping that your father will join us in marriage once we're at sea."

"Hmmm." Edwin gave a sarcastic huff. "I suppose it will make the sleeping arrangements better if you do that." He looked Rebecca up and down again. "But who knows?"

"There are mattresses and blankets on the cargo deck. I recommend that you go down and stake out your stop."

"Thank you." Rebecca could tell Joshua wanted a confrontation and pulled him away.

Once beyond earshot, Joshua whispered. "I don't like Edwin, and I don't like the way he was looking at you."

"He was just being a gentleman, Joshua." She held up the hand Edwin kissed. "That's how gentlemen greet ladies."

"I still don't like him."

With their bedding placed at the aft corner of the cargo deck and a promise to stay away from Edwin, Joshua returned to the main deck to help get the ship underway. As the last hawser was flung aboard and the sails opened for steerage, the *Maiden* began to turn away from the dock in the easy current of the Thames. Two other ships of equal length backed their sails and turned into the easy current just behind them.

"You there!" It was the soldier who had arrested Joshua. "I owe you a flogging!"

Captain Drake stepped to the rail and called back. "I'm the captain of this ship! Who are you calling to?"

The soldier pointed at Joshua. "Him! The one with that cut to his left cheek!"

"What did he do?"

"He broke a man's fingers—one on each hand—and the constable wants him for trial and a well-deserved flogging!"

The captain turned to Joshua. "Is that true, John? Did you break a man's fingers?"

"He's a pickpocket, Captain. He was stealing my food." Joshua gave the soldier an insulting gesture and called to him. "I should have broken his neck!"

The captain grabbed Joshua and bent an arm up behind his back. "Sorry, John, but I can't have a man of your cut aboard the *Maiden*." He led Joshua to the rail. "You can swim, I hope."

CHAPTER TWELVE:
Indentured to America

The *Maiden* was crowded with indentured servants from stem to stern. Most of the able-bodied men were immediately pressed into service raising and adjusting the sails while the women and children were sent below. Rebecca returned to the main deck to see where Joshua was working and spotted him and the captain at the rail.

Shocked at what she saw, Rebecca ran across the deck to them. "What's going on?"

"It seems that John—your *betrothed*—owes the constable his back for breaking a man's fingers. Is that true? Did John break a man's hands?"

"Who told you that?"

The captain held Joshua in an arm lock and nodded toward the dock. "That soldier. The one pointing at us."

"If he did, the man had it coming." She looked at Joshua. "What are you doing to him?"

"I'm about to throw him off my ship!"

"It was just his fingers." She grabbed the captain by the arm. "If he goes back, then I go back also, and you lose the credit for both of us."

"Twenty pounds each?" The captain pushed Joshua closer to the rail. "I can do without forty pounds."

"Father!" It was Edwin. "May I speak with you before you do this thing?"

"Make it quick, son. What is it?"

Edwin stepped to his father and leaned close. Joshua could only catch a word or two.

Captain Drake released Joshua's arm and called to the soldier. "If it's only a flogging he has coming, then I can take care of that at sea!" The soldier just stared back at the elderly sea captain. "Well?"

"Keep him, then! Six strokes and I'll trust that you're a man of your word!"

"I'm the captain of the *Maiden*! If a man aboard my ship deserves a flogging, then a flogging he'll get!" He turned to Rebecca and gave her a long look. "Satisfied?"

"Thank you, sir."

Captain Drake turned to one of his crewmen. "Take him below until we're gone from this place."

Edwin watched the two until they disappeared down the companionway. "Thank you, father."

"She's a commoner, Edwin, and you're a gentleman."

"Ah, yes, but what a lovely commoner. I'd wager my next month's allowance that she would clean up as good as any woman of high breeding." He gave a dirty chuckle. "With the proper training, she could attend the King's court or any fancy ball."

"But I was promised them a marriage ceremony tomorrow once we cleared the Thames into the open sea."

"Can you delay that for a few days?"

"Why?"

"For me." He gave his father a lustful smile. "Tell them that you can't marry them until we reach the open sea—the ten or twenty mile mark. Tell them it's a British maritime law or something."

"You have designs on the maiden, don't you?"

"Think about it, father. I want a wife and you want a grandchild. Rebecca Keyes is the quickest way to achieving both our desires."

The captain gave his son a questioning look. "You're asking for trouble, Edwin."

☠ ☠ ☠

A gentle southwesterly blew across London and the Thames River the entire afternoon, driving the *Maiden* along the meandering waterway ahead of the gentle current. Within an hour, the *Maiden* had passed the outskirts of southeastern London and turned through the twisting Limehouse, Greenwich, and Blackwall Reaches toward the open sea. The tackle and sheets required constant trimming through the turns, but the Thames finally straightened out, leaving Joshua some time to spend with Rebecca. He descended the ladder to the cargo hold where the women were gathered.

"Rebecca." He held up a clenched fist. "I have something for you."

"What is it?" Rebecca stepped to the ladder.

He turned his hand over and opened the fingers. In his palm lay the Ferrier's nail John Manley gave him. "John gave me this the first time I left Wakehurst. It's just a Farrier's nail, but it means a lot to me. I want you to have it."

"Why don't you give it to me when we say our vows tomorrow?"

"Because I should have given it to you when I asked you to marry me."

"You never gave it to me because you never asked, Joshua."

"I didn't?" He looked down at the ring. "Are you sure?"

"Yes!" Her tone was angry and with a touch of expectancy. "You told me that people in love indenture themselves together. That isn't the same thing as a formal proposal."

"Okay, I'll make it official." He dropped to a knee. "Rebecca Keyes, will you marry me?"

She thrust her left hand at him and spread her fingers. "Yes, Joshua Smoot. I'd be honored to marry you."

He smiled and slipped the ring onto her third finger.

She held up her hand. "It's a little large."

He pulled it off and looked at her through it. "John made it for my finger."

"I have other fingers." She held up her hand. "It must fit one of them."

He tried the middle finger, and it was still too large. Finally, he pushed it onto her thumb. "There. A perfect fit."

"I promise you that I will wear this ring until the day I die."

Joshua stood and pulled Rebecca into a long embrace. Several of the other passengers began clapping.

"When's the wedding?" It was a woman near the stern.

"Tomorrow!"

"Before or after your flogging?" Joshua spun about at the familiar voice. It was Edwin. He stood on the ladder, two steps from the bottom.

"What do you want?"

"What makes you think I want something?"

"Because in the short time we've been aboard, nothing you do is without a purpose."

"Well, John Manley, like you, I'm a determined man." He stepped off the ladder and walked aft, wound his way between and over the clutter of bedding, and finally stopped at Rebecca. He looked down at her left hand. "And unlike you, John Manley, I'm an honest man."

"What is that supposed to mean, and why do you keep saying my whole name?"

"When you two came aboard, you claimed to be engaged. But now I see you on a knee, proposing marriage, and slipping a ring onto the maiden's thumb." He took Rebecca's hand and held it up. "A polished Ferrier's nail? Not a very impressive ring, is it?"

Rebecca pulled her hand away as Joshua stepped forward with clenched fists. She grabbed his arm. "Don't, John. He isn't worth it."

"Oh, I'm worth it, my sweet Rebecca." Edwin put his hand to the hilt of his pistol and gave Joshua a quick glance. "I'm worth ten John Manley's, and I intend that you grow to appreciate that fact long before we reach Charles Town."

Joshua pulled loose from Rebecca's grip and stepped close to Edwin. "I'm warning you. Keep your distance from my Becky."

"And if I don't?"

"Stop this!" Rebecca pulled Joshua back, stepped between the two, and faced Edwin. "We have been in love for many years, and we've both understood that we would marry someday. Now that we're on our way to America —"

Edwin burst into laughter at her impassioned speech.

"What's so funny?"

"You're both so common. And you, my sweet Rebecca, are so quick to betray your lover just to keep him out of trouble." He laughed again. "I can see that this will be a most interesting crossing." He turned on a heel, strode to the ladder, climbed halfway up, and turned. "By the way, this is my father's last trip to the American Colonies. When we reach Charles Town, I will become the master of this ship." Edwin turned and in a moment was gone.

"I'll kill him if he touches you!"

"No! We have too much to lose!"

"Are you saying that I should ignore his advances—that I should turn and look the other way while he insults us?"

"We'll be married as soon as we reach the open sea. It'll be too late for him because I'll be a married woman."

"That won't make any difference to Edwin."

"Yes, it will. He's an officer and a gentleman."

"He's a man, and you're a very desirable young woman."

She looked into his eyes with a mixture of fear, anger, and admiration. "Please, Joshua. Let me handle Edwin."

"How?"

"I'm a big girl. I've dealt with the unwanted advances of both men and boys at the Carlisle Estate. If Edwin tries to touch me, trust me. I know how to handle him."

"And if you can't, what then?"

"If I call for your help, then, and only then, must you use force to protect me."

Joshua looked toward the ladder and back to Rebecca. He nodded. "I'll agree but—"

"Just promise to never leave my side." She reached up and ran a finger along the fresh wound. "I love you, Joshua Smoot."

☠ ☠ ☠

It was the afternoon of the second day that the *Maiden* left the fresh waters of the Thames River and broke into the open sea. By the fourth morning, the small ship rounded the white cliffs of Dover and had set a course of west by southwest.

"On deck, stand by to come about!"

"This will take a few minutes." Joshua started toward his assigned station but took a moment and pointed to the port anchor. "Wait there for me."

"When are you going to ask him?"

"I asked him yesterday."

"What did he say?"

"He said that we had to wait a little longer."

"A little longer? What's the holdup?"

"You there!" The captain pointed at Joshua. "Get on those tacks and sheets or I'll give you that flogging you should have had back in Lambeth!"

Joshua pointed and gave Rebecca another push. "Go! We'll talk once these sails are set!" Joshua gave her a light kiss and then trotted across the deck to join another of the indentured men who was pulling at the main sheet. Moments later, Rebecca rejoined Joshua forward.

"What did he mean by, 'a little longer'?"

"He told me that we had to be ten leagues from the English coast before he could marry us." Joshua gave the captain and his son a quick look. "I don't want to provoke either of them with my badgering."

"Didn't the captain tell you that he would marry us once we hit the open sea?"

"Yes but..." Joshua took a large breath and let it out with a frustrated huff.

"But what?"

"This is your first time at sea, isn't it?"

"What does that have to do with whether the captain is going to honor his promise or not?"

"Shipboard life is nothing like life back at the Carlisle or Wakehurst estates." Joshua spread his arms. "I spent over six weeks watching John Flint rule over the *Walrus* like a God."

"Meaning what?"

"I may be wrong, but my gut tells me that he could kill one of the crew on a whim and throw his body over the side."

"You're telling me that good men would stand by and do nothing if their captain started killing them off one by one?"

"Mutiny is a hanging offense, and I'm told that the courts always side with the captain."

Rebecca looked aft at Captain Drake and back to Joshua. "I'm not stupid."

"Then you know that Edwin has designs on you, and will do most anything to win your hand, even if it means killing me to do so."

"You worry me, Joshua."

"Don't you see it?"

Becky looked seaward and back to Joshua. "See what?"

"We've traded away seven years of our freedom for passage to America. We're slaves—no better than the horses and sheep that worked the estates where we worked."

"It was the price we had to pay to escape from what was happening in England." She gave him a pleading look. "You scare me when you talk like this."

"Scare you? What do you think I'll do, kill somebody?"

"Didn't you try to kill Lord Lyddell? Didn't you break that man's fingers? Isn't that how all this started?" Joshua turned away and looked at the passing sea. "Joshua?"

He turned and looked down at her. "It started long before that. John Flint set me on this course when I was eight years old, and if it doesn't lead me to freedom, then it's certain to lead to my death."

Rebecca slid her arms around Joshua's chest, pulled close, pressed her cheek hard against his chest, and began to sob. "Please. Ask him when he'll perform our marriage ceremony."

"I have a feeling that we may have to wait until after we reach Charles Town."

☠ ☠ ☠

The small ship responded well to the rudder and the set of the sails, running quickly before the white cliffs for the rest of the day. With the wind steady and the course set, the above deck work fell to the lookouts and the helmsman.

Below deck, in the main salon, one of the young women lay on her bed roll and screamed out as another labor pain coursed through her body.

Rebecca called. "Joshua! Take the men and children up on the main deck! This young woman is about to birth a child!"

When the labor pain finally subsided, the woman reached out and took Rebecca's hand. "My name is Mary. Mary Steward."

"I'm pleased to meet you, Mary Steward. My name is Rebecca Keyes."

"Thank you, Becky. I was so afraid I would have to do this alone."

Rebecca looked around at the other women. "Any one of these women would have helped if I weren't here. Is this your first child?"

The young woman nodded. Tears were streaming down through the dirt on her face, creating small tracks of mud.

Rebecca looked to the ladder as the last of the children reached the main deck. Joshua and two of the other men peered back down at them.

Rebecca looked back to Mary. "Is one of those men your husband?"

Mary shook her head. "I'm not married." She put a hand across her mouth and sobbed.

"Where is your home?"

"Lambeth—the southern edge. When I was found pregnant, my parents banished me."

"Where is he—the father?"

"I haven't seen him for several weeks. He was a hot-tempered man." She shook her head. "I believe that he is dead."

Rebecca leaned down and gave her an embrace and then wiped the tears from her face. "These are terrible times for all of us, Mary. Would you mind if I said a prayer?"

"I would like that very much."

The six other women, who ranged in age from 20 to 30 years, bowed their heads. "Heavenly Father, this woman is about to bring a child into a world full of hate and turmoil. Be with her, Lord, and guide our hands as this little one takes his first breath. And then, Lord, be with Mary and this child as we cross the sea to our new homes. We thank you for your many blessings and ask that you help us be faithful witnesses to the lost souls here on the *Maiden*, and those at Charles Town. We ask this in the name of our Lord and Savior, Jesus Christ. Amen."

"Amen." The other women repeated the word one at a time. As the last one spoke, Mary was gripped by another labor pain.

"Here." Rebecca raised the blanket as several of the other women gathered to help. "I'm going to have to see how far along you are."

Mary reached down and bundled her dress up around her waist, exposing her body. "You're so young, Becky. Have you done this before?"

Rebecca nodded as she examined the birth canal. "Yes—many times." The baby's head was visible. She looked up at the other women. "I'll need two strips of clean muslin and a sharp knife for the cord."

As one of the women set to tearing the strips from her petticoat, Joshua called from above as he threw his hunting knife down into the darkness. It stuck in the bottom step. "Take mine! I'd wager John Flint's black heart that none of the ladies have a sharper one."

Less than a glass passed before the little boy had passed through the birth canal and began to cry. "Well, Mary, you have a healthy son."

"Is something wrong?" Mary said through her tears. "Why can't I hold him?"

"Nothing's the matter, Mary." Rebecca held the umbilical cord in her hand." I'm waiting for the pulse to stop before I tighten the knots and sever the cord."

"I don't understand." Mary struggled up so that she could see her child. "Why must you wait?"

"The baby's blood is still coming and going from you, and I'm keeping him low so he gets as much of his own blood as possible." Rebecca smiled. "There! It stopped!" She gave the first knot a firm tug and looked up to Mary. "Our midwife explained it to me. The moment the blood stops coursing through the cord, a hole in the heart closes, sending the baby's blood to the lungs for the very first time. It's one of God's little miracles to remind us that the child is indeed his gift to us."

"You, Becky, are one of God's little miracles." In a moment, the second constrictor knot was tightened and the cord was cut. "I will always be beholden to you for this."

"It was my pleasure to be a part of this little boy's birth."

It took only a couple of minutes for Rebecca to wipe the little boy clean and to set him to suckle. Mary looked up at Rebecca as Joshua stepped off the ladder and joined them. She looked at Joshua. "Your name is John, isn't he?"

"No." He looked up the ladder to make sure Edwin was not there. "My name is Joshua."

"That's a good Biblical name. I'll name my little boy, Joshua."

Joshua and Rebecca climbed the ladder and stepped out into the afternoon sunshine. "So, you're the Carlisle midwife."

"No, silly." She reached up and touched the scar on his face. "Misses Steiner—the woman who sewed your face back together—she's everything medical on the Carlisle estate." She gave him a smile. "I grew up helping her with all the births—human and animal—so, all the girls my age have seen this a dozen times before they get married."

Joshua looked toward the companionway. "Mary's alone, isn't she?"

"Yes, sadly."

"I heard your prayer." He gave her a dark look.

"Oh?" Rebecca studied his face. "Was there something wrong with my prayer?"

"It's a false hope, because just like us, Mary and her little boy will live a life of strife and suffering, and then they will die, just like the rest of us."

"What is it about the Bible that annoys you so much?"

Joshua turned about and leaned against the weather oak. "I find it all too fantastic. The Garden of Eden, the flood to kill everybody but Noah and his family, and then God opens the Red Sea for Moses and all his people to escape from Pharaoh and his army as he crossed the Red Sea to Midian. Those things just don't happen in the real world."

"The Bible is true, Joshua. Every word of it is true."

"Then why all of that?" He pointed aft toward London. "Why does God let evil men prosper while good men perish?"

"Sin."

"That's it? Sin?"

"Men are evil, especially the ones in power—the ones who control us."

"But you tell me that your God is in control." Joshua shook his head. "From what I've seen and lived through, your God must be looking the other way."

"It's all in the Bible, Joshua. You told me that you finished the Gospel of John."

"I did! I read it like you told me. If your God loves us so much, then why does he turn his back on us?" He pointed back toward London again. "Why did he let your parents die like that, without even a decent grave?"

"You'd have to read the whole Bible." She fell silent and looked around for Captain Drake and Edwin. They were both at the helm, watching the two.

"Have you asked Captain Drake yet?"

"No but I will."

☠ ☠ ☠

On the fifth day out of English waters, Edwin walked aft to the quarterdeck where his father was taking a sighting on the sun. "It's time, father."

The captain lowered the sextant and turned to his son. "Are you sure you want to do this?"

Edwin nodded and looked to larboard where three other small ships cut through the cold waters of the Atlantic. The closest ship paralleled their course.

"That's the *Crow*. I spoke with the captain before we sailed. He's taking a cargo of the King's prisoners and African slaves to Cuba."

"Is Cuba far enough away for you?"

Edwin turned and smiled at his father. "Actually, distance won't be a factor. Once Joshua's there, he'll never live long enough to come searching for either Rebecca or me."

CHAPTER THIRTEEN
A Forced Choice

Captain Drake watched the *Crow* with disdain as it fell aft slightly, and then regained its position to lee of the *Maiden*. He turned to his son. "That's Captain Sperry on his way to Cuba with several of the King's criminals and a full load of Africans slaves to be sold on the slave block."

"I want John Manley sent across to the *Crow*, and I want him taken to Cuba."

"For breaking a man's fingers?"

"No, Father. I will have Rebecca Keyes."

"Hush yourself, Edwin." The captain nodded forward. "Manley's coming aft."

Joshua followed the weathered rail to the raised deck at the aft cabin and called. "Permission to join you at the helm!"

"Granted!" Edwin stepped aside while Captain Drake called back. "What do you need?"

"With all due respect, sir, I'm beginning to get the feeling that you do not intend to allow Rebecca and me to marry, and I want to know why."

"Come up on the quarterdeck so we don't have to yell."

"Go aft and state your business."

"Aye." Joshua stepped up on the aft castle and looked about at the other nearby ships that paralleled their course. "You told me that once we were in the open sea, that you'd perform our marriage." He spread his arms. "Am I wrong? Is this not the open sea?"

"Watch your tone, Manley."

"You told me ten leagues." Joshua took a large breath and squared his shoulders. "Can we do it now—now that we're this far from England?"

The captain turned and looked at his son, and then back to Joshua. "What say we do it on the morrow, John, immediately after you get off watch?"

Edwin cleared his throat and flashed his father a narrow look.

"Aye." Joshua nodded his agreement. "The change of the watch would be a good time." He gave another nod. "Thank you. I'll tell Rebecca."

Edwin stepped toward Joshua. "Should I assume that I am invited with everybody else?"

"Well…" Joshua gave the two a suspicious look. "It's a small ship. It would be hard to exclude anybody even if I wanted to." He turned, descended the ladder, and walked away to the forward companionway.

"You need to belay, Edwin."

"Belay what, Father?"

"If you're going to do this thing, then it must be done exactly right. John must attack you with a weapon, and there must be several witnesses." The captain touched his knife. "If you can get him to cut you, then I can charge him with attempted murder and hang him on the spot."

"No, father." Edwin looked forward to where Joshua and Rebecca were embracing. "He must live."

"I thought you wanted him dead so you could have Rebecca."

"I've thought about this and decided that if he's executed in front of her, she will never marry me." Edwin gave a slight nod and a smile. "I must have leverage."

"What kind of leverage?"

"There." Edwin turned and pointed at the *Crow*. "The way I see it, as long as Rebecca believes that John is alive, she'll have hope that someday she'll find him and they will be back together. If we execute him in front of her, she will hate me to her grave."

"Very well. You may signal the *Crow* to stay within hailing distance for a time."

Below deck, Joshua held Rebecca close, inhaling the smell of her hair.

"What did he say?" She looked up into his eyes.

"Tomorrow morning at the change of the watch."

"Oh, how I wish my mother and father could be here to witness this." She ran her hands down the harsh material of her worn dress as if she could improve its look with the touch. "I also wish I had a nicer dress."

"Maybe one of the other women has a dress you could borrow."

"Yes—there must be one." She rose onto her tiptoes, gave Joshua a kiss on the lips, and a gentle hand to his injured cheek. "God is doing this for us."

"I am almost persuaded that your God is real, Becky." He gave her a smile. "He's allowed me to escape the King's noose, and tomorrow morning, we will be husband and wife."

☠ ☠ ☠

It was a clear and sunny morning when Joshua and Rebecca climbed up onto the main deck of the *Maiden*. He was dressed in a borrowed waist coat and a pair of black shoes with large pewter buckles on the fronts. Rebecca wore one of Mary's dresses. It was made of white linen with tatting about the neck and wrists. Another woman had loaned her a doily for her head. Edwin was waiting at the top of the ladder as Rebecca emerged ahead of Joshua.

"Well, well!" Edwin stepped in front of Rebecca. Has an angel from heaven graced the *Maiden* with her presence?" Before Joshua could step between the two, Edwin had taken Rebecca into his arms. "What say you give me a little kiss—sort of a wild oat kiss—the last before you get married?" Before she could pull away, Edwin kissed her full on the mouth.

Joshua let out a cry that sounded more animal than human. Before Edwin had finished the kiss, Joshua grabbed him by the queue, threw him backwards to the deck, and pressed his knife against his throat. The crew was ready for the attack, for no sooner had the trickle of blood started to run from Edwin's throat than Joshua was knocked unconscious. When he finally awoke, he was chained, hand and foot, with blood running onto the wet deck from the wound on his scalp.

Rebecca knelt before Edwin. "Please! I beg and petition you, good sir!" She pointed at Joshua. "I know you kissed me with the best of intentions, but John only reacted like any man would react!"

"You're wasting your breath, Rebecca." Edwin raised his chin to show her where he was bleeding. "John tried to murder me, and my father has already passed judgment upon him."

"But you can't hang him! Please! Have mercy on him! We were to be married!"

"The *Maiden* is a well-disciplined ship, Miss Keyes." Captain Drake stepped forward. "Fighting between common seamen is a flogging offense, but an attack on a ship's officer earns the offender the hangman's rope."

"No! Please! I beg you!"

"You have nothing to offer my father."

Rebecca kept her eyes on the captain. "Sir! The sermon you gave Sunday last. You are obviously a believer in Jesus Christ—who He is and what He did for you on the cross?"

"Aye?"

"Then you know that God has shown His mercy to you. Please show that same mercy to my John."

Edwin leaned over to his father, brought up a hand, and whispered. His father shook his head and whispered back.

"What?" Rebecca looked from one to the other. "What did Edwin say?"

"Seems he has more sympathy for your betrothed than me."

"Then…" She turned to Edwin. "Please! Tell me that you have reconsidered!"

The captain looked to the *Crow*, which was trailing by half a league. He looked back to his son. "Are you certain of this, Edwin?"

"It depends." Edwin looked down at Rebecca.

"On what?"

"You, and the decisions you make in the next few minutes."

"What decisions? What do you want me to decide?"

"John's fate, of course--whether he lives or dies."

"You're putting his life in my hands?"

"John tried to kill me. Since I am John's victim, my father has given me the authority to decide his fate. I am giving that authority to you."

Rebecca looked to the *Crow* once more. She turned back to Edwin. "What do you want from me, Edwin?"

"I want your permission to court you until we reach Charles Town."

"Court me?"

"For the rest of this crossing, I want you to walk with me whenever the mood strikes me. I want you to eat with my father and me, and I want you to willingly accept my kisses." He stepped close to her. "When we reach Charles Town, I intend to ask for your hand in marriage."

Rebecca stared up at him in disbelief. "I will never marry you, Edwin Drake!"

"I'm not requiring that you marry me—not yet that is. I'm simply asking for a chance to change your mind."

"If I agree to your demands, what happens to John?"

"The *Crow* is taking several of the King's condemned prisoners and a full count of African slaves to the Caribbean. It will be your choice whether John Manley becomes a slave or hangs from the *Maiden's* yardarm,"

"Where will he be taken?"

"The captain of the *Crow* will be making several stops on the islands." He took her hand and pulled her to her feet. "The only thing that should matter to you is that he's alive on one of the plantations." He kissed her hand. "Better lost in the Caribbean than dead on the *Maiden*, I say."

"I agree." She looked forward to where Joshua was bound and guarded by several of the crew. "Send him across to the *Crow*."

Edwin leaned down and kissed her cheek. "Splendid!" He pulled her to her feet and handed her to his father. "How soon can the prisoner be transferred?"

Before the ship's bell struck again, a weighted monkey's fist and hauling line was thrown across to the *Crow* and secured to Joshua's chains. Edwin stepped to the opening in the rail where Joshua was being held. He held up a leather pouch that had been dipped in tallow. "This is for Captain Sperry." He put the lanyard over Joshua's head. He shoved it into Joshua's shirt. "Be sure he gets it."

Rebecca wrenched her hand loose from Captain Drake and ran across the deck to Joshua. "Where are they taking him?"

"That will be up to Captain Sperry."

"I love you, Joshua!" She reached out to him, but Edwin pushed her away. "I'll wait for you!"

"By John Flint's black heart, I swear that I will come back for you!"

With a signal to the *Crow*, the hauling line was pulled, jerking Joshua from the *Maiden* and into the cold water of the Atlantic.

CHAPTER FOURTEEN:
Charles Town Arrival

O nce pulled from the cold Atlantic, Joshua was thrown down onto the deck half unconscious and spitting up salt water. Before he could struggle to his feet, one of the seamen gave him a rough kick to turn him on his back.

"The *Maiden* signaled that you are carrying a message for Captain Sperry." The man tore Joshua's borrowed shirt open, jerked away the leather pouch that hung from his neck, and handed it to the captain.

While the crew retrieved the hauling line, Captain Sperry opened the pouch and scanned the short letter. "Well, well, John Manley. You're a truly fortunate man."

Joshua turned his head and looked up. "What did he tell you about me?"

"He says that you tried to murder his first officer over the attentions of a young woman."

"The young woman is my betrothed. Captain Drake was to marry us today."

"So, you say."

"It's the God's truth!"

"And what of this attack on his first officer? I suppose that's a lie also?"

"He's Edwin Drake—the captain's son!" Joshua struggled to stand but was pushed back down to his knees. He raised his manacled hands. "Edwin did this to me so he could have Rebecca, and then he forced her to choose these chains or my death."

"So, you say." He looked at the letter again. "While you're on your knees, you should thank the good Lord that I've agreed to do this. For some reason that I do not understand, he wants you alive at Baracoa rather than dead and hanging from his yardarm."

The captain held up the letter again. "He said you would tell me a tale of woe, and to not believe a word of it."

Joshua looked across at the *Maiden*. Edwin was still holding Rebecca's hand. "That devil exchanged my life for Rebecca's permission to court her." He looked up at this new captain. "She had no choice but to send me to you."

"Captain Drake tells a much different story." He scanned down several lines, cleared his throat, and read aloud. "John Manley is a common seaman and had been assigned to above deck duties. My first officer noticed how the young scoundrel was watching one of the young bondswomen, and when he stepped forward to protect the girl's honor, Manley attacked him with a knife." The captain looked down at Joshua. "This makes more sense than your story."

Joshua gave a low growl. "Where is Baracoa, and why would Captain Drake want me sent there?"

"That's where the Spaniards established their first town on Cuba, and that's where the Catholics burned heretics at the stake for resisted their religion."

"That's all I did to Captain Drake and his son. Edwin wanted Rebecca for himself and I fought for her."

"Like I said, that's your story." He held up the letter. "This is Captain Drake's story."

"It's a lie!"

"Lie or not, the word of a sea captain is always above the word of a lowly seaman."

"Edwin knew that if he had hung me, Rebecca would never allow him to court her."

"Ha!" The captain turned and looked to the *Maiden*. "It would have served you better if you had told Drake and his son that Rebecca was your sister."

"Like Abraham told Pharaoh?"

The captain gave Joshua a questioning look. "Abraham who?"

"The first book of the Bible. Abraham lied to the Pharaoh that his wife Sarah was his sister because he feared the Egyptian King would kill him to have her. He paid a high price for that lie, and I wasn't about to repeat it."

"The Bible. Ha!" He nodded to the two men. "Take him forward and throw him in the chain locker until I decide what to do with him."

Joshua turned, filled his lungs, and called out to Rebecca. "They're taking me to—" Before he could finish, the boson struck Joshua with a belaying pin, rendering him unconscious.

Joshua was dragged to the forward hatch and thrown down into the locker. He lay there for several minutes before his eyes fluttered open. He looked up to where Captain Sperry stood over him.

"Learn to love those chains, John Manley, because they are now your life—a life of chains and slavery."

☠ ☠ ☠

For two days the *Maiden* and the *Crow* sailed in tandem toward the New World. Out of fear that Edwin would bring back Joshua and have him hung, Rebecca accepted the young man's attention, being careful however, to neither violate her personal standards of morality and decorum, nor her sacred vows to Joshua. With a signal from Captain Drake, the *Crow* finally broke off to larboard ten degrees and reset her sails for her track toward the Caribbean Ocean.

Rebecca stood alone, balancing herself at the weather rail. She had watched the *Crow* since noon as the stained sails shrank toward the southern horizon and finally disappeared. She stiffened at the familiar sound of Edwin's footsteps as he approached from the ship's bow.

"Dinner will be at four bells, my dear." He put a hand on hers. "I trust you'll accept our invitation as usual."

She pulled her hand from the rail and turned on him like a cornered cat. "If you touch me again, I'll finish what Joshua began!"

"Are you threatening my life, Rebecca?"

"We were to be married!" She slapped his face. "You forced him into that fight, and you had already told the crew what was to happen! You and your father had it all planned!"

Edwin stepped close and sniffed at her hair. She pulled back against the shrouds and rat lines. "If you know that, then you also know that at my word, you could be hanged for the threat you just made."

"You wouldn't!"

"Reject my love, if you must." He rubbed his stinging cheek. "If you want to live to reach Charles Town, then be careful to never slap or shame me in front of my father, the other indentured passengers, or the crew."

"I agreed to let you court me, but only to save Joshua's life."

"Joshua?" He gave her a questioning look. "That's the second time I've heard you call him by that name."

"It…"

"Well? Is his name John or Joshua?"

"His name is Joshua Smoot. He is the bastard son of John Flint."

"Then his name should be Joshua Flint."

"His name was on the King's warrant list when we indentured ourselves. That's why he gave a different name."

"Ha!" He looked to the south where they last saw the *Crow*. "A fugitive of the King who will soon die as a slave." He gave a laugh. "I should have let my father hang him like he wanted—like Joshua deserved."

"If you had, then your father would have hanged me also."

"But it was Joshua who attacked me, not you."

"As God is my witness, if you and your father had killed Joshua, then I would have killed both of you before we reached the colonies."

Edwin leaned forward to give her a kiss but received another vicious slap instead. He backed away, rubbed the smarting flesh of his left cheek, and gave a laugh.

"Am I to die now?"

"No."

"But I just failed your test, and you told me that the next time I slapped you, that I will die."

"We're alone here, Rebecca. I told you to never slap or shame me in front of the others." He pointed. "Go! Make yourself ready to join my father and me at dinner."

☠ ☠ ☠

For the next five weeks, the *Maiden* sailed west among the other ships plying the trade route between Europe and the New World. The days were long and tiresome, and Rebecca cringed at the nightly dinners she had to endure with Michael and Edwin Drake.

"I'm finished." Rebecca set down her fork and wiped her mouth. "Am I excused?"

"You don't want to stay with us for a little rum?"

She glared at Edwin. "What I want is to be anywhere on this ship but at this table with you and your father."

"Very well." Edwin gave a flip of his hand. "You're excused."

Once free from the distasteful ritual, Rebecca returned to the forward hold to find Mary crying while she nursed little Joshua. "Mary?" Rebecca put a comforting arm around her shoulder. "What has happened?"

"Look at me." Marry looked up at her friend. "No husband, a bastard for a son, and a slave when I reach Charles Town." She looked down at the baby. "My pastor and all the elders told me I was a disgrace to the congregation, and that I had lost my salvation for this sin that suckles at my breast." She looked down at little Joshua. "Is my son a sin?"

"Wouldn't your parents—?"

"No. They were the ones who took me to the docks. They were as ashamed of me as the Vicar."

"They lied to you, Mary."

Mary looked at Rebecca for a long moment and shook her head. "But I did what they said I did. I gave myself to a young man when I knew it was wrong. They all told me that for a young woman, there is no sin worse than fornication." She shook her head. "I am worth nothing, and this little boy will suffer all his life for my sin."

Rebecca thought for a moment and then touched the nursing child. "Have you ever wanted something that you knew you could never afford?"

"I come from a poor family." Mary nodded slowly. "Of course, I have."

"How did you know what that thing that you wanted was worth?"

"Like always. The person who is selling something sets its price."

"But the price the person sets and the price somebody is willing to pay are seldom the same."

"That's right, Rebecca." Mary gave a squint. "A thing is only worth what somebody is willing to pay for it."

Rebecca smiled. "What did our Savior do on that cross so long ago?"

"He..." Mary blinked quickly for a moment and then smiled back at the younger girl. "He gave Himself for us. He bought us back from the Devil."

"And how much did he pay for us?"

"God paid the ultimate price—his very life."

"What does that tell you about your worth to God?"

Mary considered and smiled. "You're right, Becky. I'm worth so much to God that He would rather die than to lose me."

"Do you believe Christ's sacrifice on that Roman cross—as the Lamb of God—took away the sin of the world?"

"Yes but..."

"And the sin that brought your little boy into the world—was it taken away with the rest of mankind's sin?"

"Yes, but I'll be alone in a country with—"

"You'll be with me and your beautiful little son."

"But we'll be nothing more than slaves. How can you see any good in that?"

Rebecca gave a laugh. "Think about what is really happening to us, Mary. There was nothing left for us in England but prostitution and death. My parents were dead and your family banished you."

"But..."

"Where we're going, we'll have a place to live, good food to eat, and after seven years, we'll have a trade and know everybody in Charles Town. Trading these next seven years for all that and a new life, is a small price to pay. Actually, it's a blessing from God."

Mary switched her baby to her other breast and then looked up at Rebecca. "We'll be together in Charles Town, right? You promise that?"

"Now that Joshua is gone, I don't know where they will send me."

"You could ask to be sent where I am going." She gave Rebecca a pleading look. "Would you do that?"

"Of course, I will."

"Thank you, Becky."

"The Lord watches over His lambs. Can I do less?"

☠ ☠ ☠

The port at Charles Town was choked with Brigantines, Barks, and a medley of smaller coastal craft, forcing the *Maiden* to anchor several hundred yards out from the docks. Captain Drake and his son took one of the ship's boats to shore and made their way through the clutter of merchants to East Bay Street and the office of Sidney Baker, one of the twenty-eight King's solicitors.

The man was in his early sixties, a little heavy in the girth, mostly gray, and his cluttered office smelled of old books, sweat, and pipe tobacco. He looked over his half-glasses at the captain. "And who might you be?"

Captain Drake turned and pointed back at his ship. "Captain Michael Drake of the schooner *Maiden*." He handed the old man his manifest. "Thirty-two bond servants from Lambeth, England."

Mister Baker studied the list. "This says that you manifested thirty-three. Did you lose one at sea?"

"He was a trouble-maker. He was transferred to another ship while we were en-route."

"By agreement, you will receive twenty-five pounds for each bonded servant you deliver in good health." He took up a pencil to make the calculation.

Michael pointed to a name on the manifest. "It's eight hundred pounds. That woman—Mary Steward—had a baby after we left England. That should make up for the man we lost."

Mister Baker looked up. "Is the child indentured?"

"Obviously not, but since his mother is, then whoever takes her will get him also."

Baker put his hands to his upper chest. "Does this Mary Steward have large breasts? Enough to suckle more than one child?"

Edwin gave a chuckle from across the room. "Aye, a half-dozen from the looks of her."

"Good." He pulled a letter from a stack. "I have an immediate position for her at Doctor Peter Fayssoux's estate." The solicitor looked down the list and stopped at Rebecca. "This girl—Rebecca Keyes—you list her as a cook's assistant." He looked up at the captain. "Can you vouch for her?"

Captain Drake gave his son a quick glance. "She's a bit high-spirited but a good cook, nevertheless. She took over the duties aboard the *Maiden* when my regular cook was taken ill."

Edwin nodded. "I'll vouch for her also."

"Then both of these women will go to the Fayssoux estate." Mr. Baker made an entry in his journal. He counted out the coins and pushed them across the table.

Captain Drake scooped up the coins and dropped them into his leather shoulder bag. "There are several crates aboard my ship that are destined for the Fayssoux estate. Can you provide a wagon?"

Baker looked up at the man with a squint. "I've already sent runners to all the families who have goods on the *Maiden*. I would expect that the Fayssoux wagon is on its way as we speak."

Twenty minutes later, Edwin stepped down the companionway into the bowels of the *Maiden* and called out. "Rebecca!"

"I'm here—forward with Mary and her child."

Edwin descended the ladder and stepped over the confusion of the other passengers and their suitcases. "Get your things together—both of you. There's a wagon on the dock loading six crates of dry goods! You two will follow along to your new home." Edwin turned and climbed the ladder. He stopped, bent down, and called back. "It's silly of me to ask again, but perhaps—"

"I would marry the devil himself before I would marry you, Edwin Drake!"

"My father still needs a ship's cook. If you want to change your mind Becky, I'll pay off your indenture and you can come back."

"You know that women never crew on ships. I'm going ashore with Mary."

"Then get yourselves topside with the rest, and to hell with you!"

☠ ☠ ☠

At Rebecca's insistence, the dock hands left a spot open on the wagon so Mary and her child could ride the mile in a modicum of comfort. Rebecca rode up front with the driver.

The driver was an attractive man in his thirties. He urged the horse over the ballast-stone street to get away from the clamor of the docks, and then reined the horses to a stop on the smoother red bricks of East Bay Street. He turned to Rebecca. "My name is Grady Olsen. I am what you might call the estate's handy man. I tend to the livestock and the garden, build things, make repairs to the home as needed, and a dozen other things. I understand you are to be the new cook's assistant."

"Yes."

"Does that Farrier's nail ring on your thumb mean anything?"

"It was to be my wedding ring, but there was trouble aboard the *Maiden*. My betrothed was sold into slavery when he fought for my honor."

The man shook his head. "Do you know where he was taken?"

"No—somewhere in the Caribbean." She shook her head. "They both knew—the captain and his son—but wouldn't tell me."

"That's not good."

As they turned onto Tradd Street, Rebecca looked up at the tall homes. "Tell me about the doctor and his family."

"Doctor Peter Fayssoux is one of Charles Town's men of distinction. He went to Edinburgh University in '66 at the age of 21 and was mentored by Benjamin Rush. He came back to Charles Town in '69 and set up a very successful medical practice."

"I was told that he's married and his wife is expecting a child soon."

"Yes—her name is Natalie. Her baby is due in a few weeks."

"That's why I'm here. My milk is good and plentiful."

Grady stopped the wagon at number 126—a three-story wood frame structure with a double wrought iron gate to the left of the front door. The Fayssoux estate stood in a line of tall homes on Tradd Street between Logan and Legare Streets. It was a wood frame structure two stories tall with the kitchen on the first floor and a row of servant's bungalows in the back across from the stables. Grady whistled, bringing a young Negro from the courtyard to open the gate so the wagon could enter.

While Rebecca and Mary climbed down from the wagon, the crates were offloaded onto the bricks. In a moment, the tops were pried open and the goods were spread on the cobblestone courtyard in neat rows. There were six pairs of adult size round-toed leather shoes, four pairs of women's kid gloves, ten slim boxes filled with one pair each of silk stockings, a man's beaver hat, a great riding coat of wool, two pairs of riding breeches, a man's suit of fine broadcloth, several dozen silver eating utensils, a small box of glassware, and a larger box of fired China dinner plates.

While Grady led the horses away to the stables, a stern and wiry man in a black suit and high chalked collar stepped from the home and took the manifest in hand. As he ticked off the items, they were carried inside.

The man turned to Rebecca and Mary. "Your names?"

Rebecca stepped forward and offered her hand. "I'm Rebecca Keyes. This is Mary Steward. We are both pleased to meet you, Doctor Fayssoux."

"I'm the butler. My name is Matthew Conway. You will address me as Mister Conway." He looked to Mary. "As it is apparent that you have no husband, I must assume the child you are holding is a bastard, Am I correct?"

"Yes." Mary looked to Rebecca. "I was rejected by friends and family—the people who should have helped me. Please don't join in that rejection of me."

"It wouldn't be me, Mary Steward."

"Then...?"

"Doctor and Lady Fayssoux are devout Episcopalians." He pointed to the steeple on Saint Philip's Church. "My lady will be needing a wet nurse, but neither she, nor the master will tolerate a bastard in their home. Therefore, I will tell them that you were a married woman when you embarked from England, and your husband died at sea." He gave Mary a questioning raise of his brows.

Rebecca gave the man a penetrating look. "They would rather live with an open lie than a bastard?"

"They will never know it to be a lie." There was an icy finality in Conway's voice. He looked at Rebecca. "What about you? I assume that since you came alone and you have no wedding ring that you are single."

"I…" She gave Mary a quick look. "Yes—I'm unmarried."

He looked back to Mary. "Well?" She hesitated. "If you have difficulty with that, I will make other arrangements for you."

"Other arrangements?" Mary gave Rebecca a worried look. "What kind of *other* arrangements?"

"I will notify Doctor Fayssoux that neither of you will do. There are many ships arriving daily with young women who would sell their souls to come here to be a cook and or a wet nurse."

Mary gave Rebecca a terrified look. "I need this position, Mister Conway." She gave Rebecca another look. "Please. We can keep our mouths shut as well as the next person."

Rebecca stepped in front of Mary. "Answer my question, sir. Do your master and lady want liars working for them?"

Mary put her hand to Rebecca's arm. "Please don't, Becky. It's his lie, not ours."

Rebecca gave the butler a nod. "Very well. But if anybody else asks us, we'll tell them to ask you."

Conway smiled and beckoned for them to enter a door at the back of the large home. "This is our cook, Margaret." The cook, a heavy-set woman in her forties, gave the two a forced smile and a nod. "Margie, this is Rebecca Keyes and Mary Steward. Rebecca will be your new assistant and Mary will be Lady Fayssoux's wet nurse and her child's nanny."

"Oh, you have a baby." The cook set down her mixing spoon and wiped her hands on the towel at her waist. "How old is she?"

"*He's* five weeks."

Margaret pulled down the blanket to see the baby's face. "Well, with the color of those clothes, one shouldn't be expected to know, would one?"

Mary shook her head.

The cook reached out and gave Mary's breast a squeeze. "Then you'll be Lady Fayssoux' wet nurse and nanny when she births."

Mary pulled away at the unwelcome touch. "Yes, ma'am."

Margaret turned to Rebecca. "So, Rebecca, tell me about your experience at shopping and cooking."

"I grew up doing that on an estate near Lambeth, England."

"Well then, I might send you to the market with a pocket of money and a shopping list in the morning." Margie gave Rebecca a look from head to foot. "You look solid enough to push a cart to the market, but I'd suggest some lighter clothes."

Rebecca read down the list and pushed it into her pocket. "This—these things I'm wearing—is all I have."

"Left London in a rush, did we?"

"I have several changes of clothes." Mary gave Rebecca a touch. "We'll do fine."

Conway recognized the difficult moment and cleared his throat. "The housekeeper—Miss Taylor—will have some clothes for both of you."

Margaret's tone became sarcastic. "If she can get her priorities straight, she might."

"Where is Miss Taylor?" Conway looked toward the dining room. "Is she up with Lady Fayssoux?"

"I believe she's out at the stables helping Mister Olsen with the horses." She gave a disgusted huff. "You know, of course, that the two are getting quite serious."

"What our housekeeper and footman do is none of your business, Margie. Yours is to provide the family and your fellow servants with healthy and nutritious meals, and nothing more."

Margret gave Rebecca and Mary a quick glance. "Of course, it's none of my business." She gave another frustrated huff. "Nothing that happens around here is any of my business."

Conway turned to Rebecca. "Rebecca, would you walk across the court-yard to the stables and fetch the housekeeper? She's the tall woman with red hair."

Becky nodded. "Of course." She turned and walked out into the sunlight. The stable doors were open and secured back, allowing the familiar smell of urine and horse manure to drift out across the cobblestones to the young girl. She stepped to the door and found the two kissing. Rebecca cleared her throat, catching their attention. "Mister Conway asked me to find you, Miss Taylor. I'm one of the two new indentured servants from England—Rebecca Keyes."

The housekeeper was a woman in her early thirties, with auburn hair to her shoulder blades, light skin, and fine features. If she had been dressed in finer clothes, she would pass as Lady Fayssoux at even the finest Charles Town balls.

The woman smiled and walked to Becky. "Welcome to the Fayssoux Manor, Rebecca. Have you met the cook yet?"

"Yes, ma'am." She gave a smile. "Margaret seems to be a very nice lady."

"This is Grady Olsen, the footman."

"We rode from the docks with him."

Miss Taylor stepped next to Grady and took his hand. "If the cook has not already told you, Mister Olsen and I are in love and plan to be married soon."

"Yes, she did mention your relationship." Rebecca gave the man a smile. "Grady and I had a good talk on our way from the docks."

The housekeeper took Rebecca by the arm. "Let's step outside, dear." She stopped next to a wrought iron table and chairs. "Margie is a good cook and a diligent worker, but she is a consummate gossip. Never—even if you have no-body else with whom to share a problem—confide in the woman. To do so is to spread your personal business through the house and most of Charles Town within an hour."

"We had one like her at Weir Wood."

"Weir Wood? That's only six or seven furlongs south of Lambeth."

"Do you know England?"

"I was born in Lambeth. My parents brought me to Charles Town when I was ten."

"We…" Rebecca's voice caught.

"What is it?"

"My betrothed was taken from me en-route here. We were to be married, but…"

"Taken? Was he killed?"

"No." She hardened. "I sent him away as a slave."

"You sent the man you were to marry into slavery?"

"The captain of the *Maiden* and his son conspired against us to get rid of Joshua."

"How? What did they do and why did they do it?"

"The captain's son—Edwin Drake—wanted me for himself and forced Joshua into a fight. The captain was going to hang him from a yardarm, but I begged for his life." She began to sob. "They gave me a choice."

"Slavery or death." Susan put a comforting arm around Rebecca. "Are you a believer, Rebecca?"

"Oh, most assuredly."

"Then you must trust the Lord to bring him back to you someday." Rebecca nodded. "How long are you willing to wait for him?"

"All my life, or until I am convinced that he is dead."

CHAPTER FIFTEEN:
The Marketplace

Rebecca and Miss Taylor walked across the courtyard to where Mary was waiting with her baby and their bags. The housekeeper extended a hand to Mary. "Welcome to Fayssoux Manor. My name is Susan Taylor. I'm the housekeeper."

Mary bowed her head as trained to do when in the presence of her superiors. "I am very pleased to meet you, Miss Taylor."

The housekeeper shook her head and gave the young woman a mother's expression of sympathy and disappointment. "There'll be none of that with me, young lady. I'm a fellow domestic, not your employer. My first name is Susan and that's how I wish to be addressed."

"But—"

The housekeeper held up a hand. "As you'll presently discover, there are no persons of royal blood in the colonies, even though many believe themselves to be bluebloods."

Rebecca tilted her head. "But indentured servants—like Mary and me—have to know their place, don't they?"

"It's called civility and good manners. Even the Generals and Statesmen—if you should meet them when you are sent to the marketplace—will treat you with kindness and respect, provided they are true gentlemen."

"We can call you Susan when we are about our work but…" Mary gave the woman a worried look. "Surely we should show you more respect in the company of the doctor and Lady Fayssoux."

"Very well, but that is the only time that you will address me as Miss Taylor."

Rebecca smiled and gave an almost imperceptible nod. "Then for the sake of safety, we would prefer to call you Miss Taylor at all times."

"If you choose." Susan escorted the two young women past the kitchen, through a narrow hallway, and to a small room at the back of the house with a single window that looked out onto the courtyard. "I know it's small for two, but it's all we can spare. Mary, you will stay with Rebecca until Lady Fayssoux is due, and then you and your baby will move into the nursery with her baby."

Rebecca looked about the room. And then this room will be mine?"

"Yes, if you don't mind being alone."

Rebecca set her bag on the bed to the right and looked around. The room measured ten by twelve feet and there were two medium wardrobes, matching desks, and two single beds—one against each wall.

"This is wonderful." Rebecca turned about. "Our entire cottage at Weir Wood was not much larger than this, and there were three of us."

Mary set her baby on the bed. "I grew up in a loft house smaller than this." She pointed at the ceiling. "We cooked and ate in a room this size and our beds were up in the rafters."

"I'm pleased that you like it." Susan stepped to the door and stopped. "You've both had a long sea crossing, so the rest of this day is yours."

Rebecca pulled the cook's list from her pocket and held it out to the woman. "But the cook told me that I'm to take this list to the market as soon as I put my things away."

Susan shook her head and took the list. "Tomorrow morning will be soon enough for that. Right now, you both need a long-overdue bath, your clothes need washing, and you need to eat something. You do have a change of clothes, right?"

"We do."

"I'll tell the cook to fix you something to eat, and then I suggest you go for a walk about Charles Town to get your bearings. There's quite a bit to see."

"But we've never been here before."

Susan gave Mary a motherly smile. "I'll prepare you a map and draw a line to the marketplace. And then you'll want to see some of the shops along the docks."

Mary gave a questioning tilt of her head. "What will my duties be until Lady Fayssoux's baby is born?"

"I will introduce you to Lady Fayssoux in the morning after breakfast. As you are aware, she is nearly ready to birth. Since you have so recently given birth, she will be pleased to have you as a personal friend and confidant."

"I…" Mary gave Rebecca an unsure look. "I'm just a country girl."

Susan gave Mary a comforting smile. "I assume you are also a believer."

"Oh, yes." Mary gave Rebecca a quick glance. "I can't remember a time when I did not believe in Jesus Christ and what he did for me on the cross."

"Doctor and Lady Fayssoux are believers also. Just be respectful to her wishes and be her friend."

"When you say that I'll be a confidant—"

"It means that anything she discloses to you will be strictly between you and her unless she tells you otherwise. Guard that intimacy well, for it will be your secrets that are kept also."

"I've helped delivered the young of many farm animals but never a human baby." Mary gave Rebecca a quick glance. "Becky has more experience at midwifery than I do."

Susan laughed. "We have several doctors with birthing skills, and very capable midwives here in Charles Town. Lady Fayssoux will have the best of care when her time comes."

"And then I will nurse the baby."

She looked at Rebecca. "Since you will be working in the kitchen and doing most of the shopping, I suggest that when you get to the market that you meet as many of the merchants as you can. Let them know who you work for and that you will not tolerate anything but honest dealings." She looked at Mary. "It's seven or eight blocks to the market—a fifteen-minute walk—so I'll get you a perambulator for your child."

Rebecca took Susan's hand. "Thank you for all this. The Lord has given Mary and me a new life and a wonderful new family."

An hour later, after both women had taken a bath, put on their fresh clothes, and eaten, they set out to explore the town. As directed, they walked through the yard to the narrow alleyway that snaked its way between the adjacent homes and out to Legare Street. Using the map Miss Taylor had provided, Becky and Mary followed Dock Street east and turned left onto East Bay Street.

The docks along the Cooper River were teaming with merchants who were hawking their wares while able-bodied seamen competed for the rare and high-paying openings on the barks or brigantines that were departing daily for England.

Two and three-story homes stood in a neat row on the west side of East Bay Street facing the clutter of ships. To the women's right, huddled beneath the tangle of bowsprits crouched the brothels and taverns that robbed the seamen of their hard-won wages. Men, with no apparent purpose in life except to look menacing, sat about the street watching the two passing ladies. Rebecca recognized the danger and pulled Mary back to the left sidewalk.

"We'll do far better on this side of the street, Mary."

Mary looked across at four seamen who were watching them from under a workman's awning. They had the demeanor of a pack of hungry dogs. "Yes." She gave a shudder. "I believe you're right."

The two stepped quickly past Queen Street and in minutes were at Cumberland. Rebecca looked at the map and pointed. "That's the market just ahead." All manner of wagons, carts, and other miscellaneous contrivances for carrying goods to and from the docks cluttered Market Street and the entrance to the eastern end of the first building.

An elderly black woman with woven sea grass hats and baskets stepped in front of Mary. "Ah-ha!" She pulled a briarwood pipe from between stained teeth and spoke with a gravelly voice. "Tis a new mother with a new babe!" She pulled a wide brimmed hat from behind her back and placed it on Mary's head. "My name be Tully. You shouldn't be exposin' that fair face o' you's to Old Man Sun." She put a hand to her wrinkled face. "Why, you be agin' faster dan a prune, an' in no time you be lookin' as old as Tully, you will!"

Mary took off the hat and held it out to the woman. "I don't have any money. Rebecca and I just arrived from England this morning."

"Ah-ha!" The black woman looked at Rebecca and back to Mary. "You be slaves or bond servants!"

"We're bond servants. Our housekeeper sent us here."

"Then you's been sent to buy food and not hats."

Mary gave a nod. "Our housekeeper told us—"

Rebecca pushed the hat back into the woman's hand. "We were told to look over the market, meet the merchants, and find the best deals for our master and lady. I'll be back tomorrow with a hand cart to buy what we need."

"Well, well! This here jus' happin' to be yer lucky day, 'cause old Tully knows everybody in the market!" She stepped close to Rebecca. "You tell me who dat master an' dat lady be, an' Tully show you 'round!"

"No thank you." Rebecca backed away from the woman's smell. "We wish to meet the merchants on our own."

"Den at the least, tell Tully what yer master does fo' a livin'."

"We don't know what he does."

"Well, you watch yo'self, 'cause half'a dem be scoundrels, an' t'other half'll cheat ya three ways ta Sunday next."

Rebecca held up a hand while she and Mary backed away. "Please."

The woman hooked the hat's lanyard behind her arm and held up a hand. "You two'll be back for Tully's help. You'll see!"

As the two stepped away, Mary whispered. "I saw a few Africans in Lambeth, but none of them were at all like her."

"She's my first too." Rebecca looking back at the noisy woman. "Friendly enough but quite frightening if one isn't prepared for her."

Just inside the eastern most building, the two young women stopped and marveled at the confusion. Neither of the girls had seen anything quite like what lay before them. The four buildings stood forty feet wide and stretched for three blocks—the shortest at 130 feet and the longest at 530 feet. The carts moved east and west to either side of the buildings, with merchants competing for the empty spaces where they could tie up their horses. There was a lot of shoving and yelling between the various merchants as they unloaded and carried their goods into the long market buildings from their open ends and the side openings along North and South Market Street. There seemed no rhyme or reason for what was placed where. A fishmonger would stand next to a tinker or a tailor, and then there would be a smithy selling wrought iron hinges beside them.

Men yelled at each other over their heavy loads while others laughed and swore like the sailors aboard the *Maiden*. A toddler was crying somewhere further inside the market and calling for his mommy. Two men haggled over several bolts of cloth in the French language. There was laughter, like what would roll out onto the roadway from a sailor's tavern, while solicitors wrote contracts on sheets of parchment.

The smells were as confusing as they were varied—fresh soil and the vegetables that grew in the loam, fancy-dressed ladies pulling their perfumed dogs on decorated leashes, the stinking bodies of the laborers mixed with the horse droppings, the tables and bins of flowers, and leather goods. Across from the solicitors sat three children stitching and filling sugar bag dolls with oats, barley, or beans. The carts never stopped coming and going, and neither did the yelling and laughter. Nearly every corner had a beggar—some old, some blind, and others missing an arm or a leg.

Mary pushed her perambulator into the first building and stopped to look at a woman who was busy tatting a small hat.

The woman looked up at Mary. "How old is your baby?" She leaned close so she could see into the perambulator.

"Five weeks tomorrow. He was born on the ship one week out of Lambeth."

"Let me guess. You two indentured yourselves to get here." The two nodded. "That means neither of you have any money, right?" Mary shook her head. The woman reached into a woven bag at her side and pulled out a blue crocheted hat. She pushed it carefully onto little Joshua's head. "Can an old lady give your baby boy a belated birthday present?"

Mary nodded. "Thank you. That's so kind."

"Have you been sponsored yet?" Rebecca began to answer, but the woman continued. "I belong to the Lady's Guild at Saint Philip's Episcopal Church. We help young women to get on their feet. If you need clothes or a place to stay for a night or two, we can help."

"We do have a place and food." Rebecca gave the woman a smile. "We're servants for the next seven years at an estate toward the south of town. My name is Rebecca. I'm to be the cook's assistant, and Mary will be our mistress's nanny."

"Well then, I expect to see you here often, Rebecca." The woman gave a warm smile and went back to her tatting.

As the two walked away from the woman, a thin man in his late twenties touched Rebecca's arm. He smelled of fish. He pointed to a cart across the way. "I have fish for sale at three cents each."

Rebecca whispered to Mary. "I don't know if that's a good price."

Mary turned around to the man. He was handsome but gaunt. "How large are the fish, and how fresh?"

He ushered them across the aisle to his cart where several dozen fish lay on oil cloth. "They're as fresh as anybody can get them, and they all come about the same size."

Rebecca shooed away several flies and touched the closest fish. "Their eyes are glazed over. How long have they set here?"

The man glanced at two Negroes twenty feet away. They were selling fish identical to his. "My name is Samuel Paine. I have a wife and a two-year-old baby girl. Not three months ago I completed my time as a bond servant and was released. I had a little money—enough to pay for this spot in the market and buy some fish at the docks." He turned and looked at the Negroes. "Those two are selling fish for a penny less than anybody else in the market because they're slaves of a fishing captain. I must be honest. I can't compete with their prices."

Rebecca thought for a moment. "I'm to be back tomorrow morning around ten o'clock with money and a shopping list. If you can sell me live fish, I'll pay five cents each."

"Live fish?" Samuel looked east toward the docks. His eyes darted about for a moment. He looked down at his cart. He began to nod and smile. He looked up at Rebecca. "I could put up sides on my cart, line it with oil cloth, and fill it with sea water."

"I will be buying six fish like those. If you can have them here and still swimming at ten in the morning, I'll buy them, Sam Paine."

"Yes. I'll be here waiting for you."

"Look!" Mary pointed to a table with English pottery. "We had a full setting of that design before we were put out of our home and off the land." She touched a cup and saucer and gave the lady a look.

"Of course, you can pick it up."

Mary raised the cup and turned it over. "This could have been ours—the very setting we had to leave behind."

"Uh…we best be moving on, Mary. There are a few men across the way looking at us."

"Oh?" She looked where Rebecca gave a tilt of her head. "That one to the right is quite easy on the eyes."

"Mind yourself, Mary. That attitude is what got you into this."

"But now that I'm here, I need a husband."

"We both need husbands, but I'm certain that neither Doctor Fayssoux nor his wife would approve of us shopping for one here—the place where people buy and sell their wares."

"So, if they smile at us, we shouldn't smile back?"

"This is our first day in Charles Town, and our first time at the market. Let's give ourselves some time to figure out they lay of the land, as they say."

"Alright." Mary gave the man in the brown coat a quick glance to make sure he was still watching her."

It took Mary and Rebecca another hour to tour the four market buildings. As they walked out of the last building, they headed down Church Street toward the Fayssoux estate.

Mary stopped next to the sign in front of a tall church. "This is Saint Philip's Episcopal Church. Do we have time to see whether any of the guild ladies are here?"

Rebecca gave a nod and touched her dress. "Of course, we have time. I could use a dress too, if they have one to spare."

An hour later, the young women were nearing the estate. The housekeeper was walking down through the alleyway with Grady and called out. "Back already?" The couple stepped to the two young women. "I didn't expect you two until closer to dark."

"Rebecca's going to buy six live fish tomorrow at the market."

"Live fish?" Grady gave a questioning tilt of his head. "They're doing that now?"

"No, but we met a man who thinks he can work it out. I told him I'd pay extra for live fish."

"Well done, Rebecca." He gave a nod of approval. "You're going to fit in here very well."

CHAPTER SIXTEEN:
Joshua and Simbatu

*J*oshua awoke to the familiar sound of the hatch bolt being pulled out of the keeper above him. It was nighttime. He expected the worst and held a hand across his face for protection. A lantern illuminated the left side of a crewman's face.

"Those chains can't be very kind to your back." The voice was rough, and just above a whisper. "I figured you'd like a piece of sail cloth and a couple of blankets."

"Thank you."

"A question, John Manley."

"You want to know what I did on the *Maiden* to deserve this."

"I've never seen my captain do this to a white man—slave or free."

"Captain Drake and his son staged a fight to get rid of me so they could take the girl I was to marry."

"So, this is your punishment for simply protecting the girl you loved?"

"Yes." Joshua studied the man. "Who are you?"

"Nobody." The man looked around the deck and back down at Joshua. "I'm just one of the crew offering a bit of Christian charity to a man in need." The man threw the pieces of cloth down to Joshua.

"Wait! Don't leave!" Joshua took a large breath. "Your name?"

"It's best you don't know my name."

"Why?"

"Because Captain Sperry wants you to suffer, and if he finds out that I gave you this, I could be punished."

Joshua held up the three pieces of cloth. "For these?"

"I know it's not much, but it's best you don't know my name in case he finds out and asks you who gave them to you." The man stood and put a hand to the hatch. "I have to go."

"Wait!"

"What?"

"There was another man—his name was Jasper—who showed me kindness like you have done."

"What about him?"

"He paid with his life for his charity to me, and I was forced to watch his flogging."

"The most Captain Sperry would do is cuss me out for giving you those things."

Joshua held up the canvas and blankets. "Thank you for these." The hatch closed as quickly as it had opened. As the bolt slid back into the keeper, Joshua folded the sail cloth to size, laid the blankets on top, and positioned the stack in the hollow he had made between the chains and the hull. It wasn't much, but it would make the rest of the voyage easier to bear.

The days and nights passed with agonizing tedium. He received two meals a day, each at the change of the watch. They consisted of a gallon of murky water, boiled cornmeal, and stewed yams—the same as the African slaves got below deck. There was no provision for his waste, except to use the food bowl or to allow it to fall amongst the chains. After three days and nights, several of the crew complained about the stench coming from the bow, so Joshua's keeper went to the captain.

"Begging your pardon, Captain, but the crew is complaining about the stink coming from the chain locker. A few buckets of water would wash Manley's filth overboard down and out through the scupper."

"Very well, Parker. You have my permission to throw as many buckets of sea water into the locker as needed to wash the mess out to sea."

At first, Joshua considered the daily dowsing's a torture but quickly realized that it was for his good.

☠ ☠ ☠

On the fourth day after being thrown down into the chain locker, the man Joshua called Angel opened the hatch and stood for several moments in silence. Joshua feared the worst.

"What has happened?"

"Things have changed."

"Am I to be flogged and thrown overboard?"

"No."

"You normally throw a bucket of seawater down on me to wash away my filth, and then give me a bowl of stewed yams or boiled cornmeal. What has changed?"

"Captain Sperry wants you brought to the quarterdeck."

"Why?"

"He'll tell you." The man held up a rope. "But first, you need to be cleaned."

"Cleaned?" Joshua pushed himself up with a grunt, stumbled slightly, and held up his arms. "I have laid in my own dung for these four days. It will take more than a bucket of seawater to clean me."

"Climb up here and hold out your hands."

"What are you going to do to me?"

"You'll see." While Joshua climbed up onto the deck, the man formed a loop near the end of a hemp rope and then folded it over upon itself, forming a knot that resembled a clove hitch. "Your hands." Obediently, Joshua put his hands through the loops and watched as the man cinched the knot tight.

"I've seen this knot before. It's a constrictor knot that the millers use to tie bags of flour so they won't spill."

"We call it a transom knot." He watched Joshua struggle to loosen it. "You're wasting your time, Manley. That knot won't give way until I allow it."

"I don't understand. I stink of my own filth, and you don't trust me to face the captain without being bound like this."

"Come." The man began to pull Joshua aft but stopped and turned. "My name is Parker." He turned and pulled Joshua to the break in the lee rail. While Joshua watched, Parker tied the other end of the rope to the rail using a bowline.

"What are you doing?"

"I'm cleaning you before you speak with Captain Sperry."

With a kick, Joshua was pushed out and into the passing sea. The thirty-foot rope snapped taught and Joshua was dragged—spinning over and over like a piece of bait on a fish hook. The cleansing took only moments.

"There!" Parker hauled him back to the rail and onto the deck. "Now you're clean and ready to speak with the captain."

Joshua struggled to his feet and held up his hands. "Does your captain fear me this much?"

"Hold still." Parker pulled his knife and sawed at the knot. "Once a transom knot is tight and wet, the only way to release it is with a knife." Once the knot released, Parker turned to the bowline tied to the rail. "This knot, on the other hand, releases as a good knot should." He turned and pointed aft. "Go."

Captain Sperry watched the entire episode and stepped forward. "Good afternoon, John Manley!"

Joshua walked to the quarterdeck and looked up at the man. "Parker said you wanted to see me."

"Have you ever crewed on a ship like this?"

"I crewed on the *Maiden* for three days before I was sent across to you."

"You claim that Captain Drake gave your betrothed a choice concerning your life."

"Aye—slavery or the noose."

"I'm now offering you a choice." Joshua did not answer. "I have allowed the other five English prisoners to choose their shackles with the Africans or to work above deck as crewmen. You can crew for me, or you can go back to your chains."

"You want me to help sail the *Crow* to Cuba?"

"That, and other duties that a ship like this requires." The captain gave Joshua a long look. "You'll stand watch like the rest of the crew, but most of your time will be spent tending to the slaves."

"I…"

"When you were in England, you tended to livestock, right?"

"Yes—mostly the horses."

"Then you'll do fine, because those Africans are nothing but livestock to be fed, exercised, and mucked."

It took Joshua a long moment to answer. "Will I eat with the crew or with the slaves?"

"Ha!" Sperry gave Joshua a smile. "Tired of slave food already, are you?"

"Yes."

"Very well. Until we reach Cuba, you will live like the rest of my crew— no better and no worse. But be warned, John Manley. Do not speak with the slaves, give them anything, and do not befriend them. As I'm certain you know, making any livestock a pet never goes well for either the man or the beast."

Joshua thought of Emily as he listened. "Are you saying that I must be mean to them like you've treated me these four days and nights?"

"No. What I'm telling you is that when you treat one of their kind like a pet, it will give them a false hope of freedom that you cannot give them." He paused and spoke slowly. "If those Africans had a soul, then I could not do what I do—buy them from the Muslims, chain them together naked, and force them to lie in their own filth for nearly two months, and then sell them to the plantations in Cuba." He paused and then spoke the words slowly. "Be assured, John

Manley. If you disobey my orders concerning these slaves, you, and the ones you befriend will suffer grave harm for it. Do you understand me?"

"What kind of harm?"

The captain turned to Parker. "Take him below and teach him his duties."

☠ ☠ ☠

Captain Sperry was correct. Tending to the Negroes was much like tending the livestock at Lord Wakehurst Place. Joshua learned his duties quickly. Every day at the change of watch, Joshua and Parker carried the two large pots of boiled rice and stewed yams to the main deck. Then he would join the rest of the crew below to unshackle the slaves so they could climb up into the fresh air and sunlight where they were forced to jump up and down for an hour to earn their food and water. While the slaves were thus occupied, Joshua and the other five English prisoners scraped and swabbed the sleeping platforms of the human waste to diminish the chances of a cholera breakout.

After a month aboard the *Crow*, Joshua was busy replacing the ankle shackles near the forward platforms when he heard a whisper. "John Manley."

"Who said that?" Joshua stood and looked toward the port side of the hold where the whisper seemed to come from. "One of you speaks English and said my name. Show yourself." He gave one of the men a pole. "Was it you?" The man just looked at him, so he poked the next man. "Did you whisper my name?"

Parker called from the stern section of platforms. "What's wrong, Manley? Is another one of them kicking at his chains?"

"No!" Joshua secured another ankle to the shackle. "Just complaining to myself!"

"Save your complaints for Baracoa where you'll need them!"

"That's the fifth time you've warned me about the place, Parker!" Joshua locked the last shackle and walked aft to the man. "What's wrong with Baracoa?"

"Nobody—slaves or indentures—last very long at the place, and the man who runs the auction doesn't pay much for replacements. That's why Captain Sperry always bypasses Baracoa and takes all his Negroes to Havana, Puerto Escondido, and Matanzas."

"What do you mean that they don't last very long? What happens to them?"

"Disease but mostly their harsh treatment—the things that kill a man or drive him to either run away or kill himself." Eight bells rang out above. "That's the change of the watch. Finish up here, Manley, and then go back and scrub the kettles."

On the forty-fifth day of the *Crow's* trip, the top watch reported that *Hispaniola* was falling aft. That told everybody that they would arrive at Baracoa the next day.

"Manley!"

"Yeah—I heard."

"I did what you asked me to do, Manley, but the captain wouldn't repent."

"So, tomorrow I become a slave again, and I'm to be sold at Baracoa to be auctioned to the highest bidder."

"Honest, Manley. I told the captain that you were a good man—that we should disregard Captain Drake's instructions and make you a permanent part of our crew."

"What if I go to him? Do you think he might change his mind if I offer to work for half pay?"

"You would do that—work for half pay?"

"Yes, to be a free man."

"If you're serious, I'll go to him now with that offer." Parker put his key in his pocket, climbed the ladder but stopped half way and pointed aft. "When you finish that last row, come up and we'll talk some more about this before I go to him."

"Yeah—I'll be up in a few minutes." While Joshua inserted his key into the next shackle, the Negro sat up and whispered his name for the second time. "It's you! You speak English!" The man stared at him for a long moment before nodding. "Are you the only one?"

"Yes, John Manley. I am the only one."

"Who are you?" Joshua turned and searched the hold for the other crewmen. There were none. "How is it that you know my language?"

"My name is Simbatu. I am an Ethiopian Jew—the son of the chief of my tribe. The Mohammedans came without warning—all with pistol, rifles, and their curved swords. They took many of the young men and women in that first raid. We knew they would come back for the rest of use, so we ran from our village to hide."

"Mohammedans? What is a Mohammedan?"

"It is the religion of the Ishmaelites and Edomites. They are the Arabians—the dwellers of the deserts."

"What deserts?"

"The deserts of North Africa and Arabia—the lands of the Egyptians and Midianites."

"So, they came back for the rest of you?"

"Yes." Simbatu was silent for a long moment, and then took a large breath. "Do you know about the Jews?"

"Yes, the Bible stories about Abraham, Isaac, and Jacob. But you were telling me how you came to be on this slave ship."

"From the time before Jesus, our people were artisans, craftsmen, masons, and carpenters for the Romans. Our villages were around Gondar and Dembiya and we were called Beta Israel." Simbatu paused. "Although we were not there when it happened, the Roman siege of Masada gave us a burning hunger for freedom."

"What is Masada?"

"Masada is a mountain next to the Dead Sea in Israel—one of the three fortresses built by King Herod to protect him from his perceived enemies."

"Go on."

"When Rome destroyed Jerusalem in 70 A.D. and enslaved the survivors of the attack, there were several pockets of Jewish holdouts. One group of these rebels—a thousand men, women, and children, called themselves the Zealots, and fled to Herod's abandoned mountain top fortress where there remained dozens of storehouses of food and a deep cistern that collected rain water. There was enough so they could have lived on Masada for a decade or more."

"Then they trapped themselves on the mountain—an easy victory for Rome, I assume."

"Not so." Simbatu shook his head. "Rome had a policy that demanded the utter surrender of every last person in a conquered nation, but Masada had only one entrance at the top of an exposed foot path that could be protected by a single man with a bow and a supply of arrows."

Joshua gave a tilt of his head.

"A multi-year siege under the supervision of the Roman General Silva began and ended with the building of a huge ramp on the western side of Masada. They pushed up a huge battering ram and when it began pounding against the wall atop Masada, the Jews committed suicide—each father killing his wife and children."

It took Joshua several moments. "The Zealots chose death over chains and slavery?"

"Yes." Simbatu nodded and looked at his shackled feet. "Unlike them, I chose chains and slavery over death." He looked up at Joshua as a tear rolled from his eye. "I was asleep with my family when they came for us."

Joshua scanned him for wounds. "Did you fight?"

Simbatu shook his head. "My father—our chief—made a deal with the Mohammedans for his life. He sold many of our people into slavery to save himself."

"Did your father sell you?"

"No, only the young men and women from the other families. That last night, when so many were killed, the Mohammedans killed my father and some of his wives at the same time."

"They killed your father after he made an agreement with them?"

"That is the way of the Mohammedans. Lying to the infidel is part of their religion."

"But you fought them, didn't you?"

Simbatu shook his head. "I did something very wrong. The others looked to me for leadership. With the death of my father, they said I was now their chief. They asked me to stand up to our captors, but I was too afraid to stand."

"But you said they had rifles and pistols. They would have killed you."

"They killed the missionaries first, and then sorted through those of us who remained. They only wanted the men and women of child-bearing age." He spread his arms. "I was to be the next chief of my people, and instead, I acted like a cur dog." He reached down and touched the shackle. "More than any of my people, I deserve this."

"What did they do with the rest?"

"Those who had not run into the jungle were killed—cut down with the large knives—like wild dogs."

"So, it was the Mohammedans—the Arabians who sold you to Captain Sperry?"

Simbatu nodded. "The Mohammedans drove us to the sea where we were put in cages until the ships came for us." He paused while the memories of that bloody night coursed through his body. "Until this thing happened to me, my name was Batu, which means freedom. Now my name is Simbatu."

"You changed your name?"

He nodded. "Simbatu means captive—no longer free. I shall carry this name until I am once again a free man." Simbatu looked down at his shackles. "I am here because I am a coward who betrayed my people."

"No. We are here because God hates you as much as he hates me"

Simbatu shook his head. "No, my friend. God loves all humans—both you and me—and even the evil men who did this to us."

"You call this love?"

"God loves you whether or not you believe it, and he went to that Roman cross to take away the sin of the world." He gave a nod. "I have answered your question—what brought me to this slave ship. Now it is your turn to tell me what brought you."

"Well, well!" It was Captain Sperry. "What have we here?"

Joshua jumped back—startled. "I was only…"

"Yes?"

"He said my name, and all I did was ask him how he knew English."

"Of all the men, women, and children I've known in my forty years, you are without a doubt the must unlucky person I've ever met."

"I didn't mean any—"

"Silence!" Sperry raised his pistol and held out his hand. "Give me your key!" Joshua handed the captain his shackle key and stepped back. "I just had an interesting conversation with seaman Parker about your future. He convinced me that I should ignore Captain Drake's instructions to sell you at Baracoa, and make you part of the crew. I repented of what I was going to do to you, and I came down here to tell you the good news." He pointed the pistol at the Negro. "Now I catch you talking with one of the slaves when you knew the penalty for doing so."

"I meant no harm, Captain."

"Well, John Manley, unlike you, I keep my word. I warned you that to disobey me would bring harm upon you and any African you befriend." He stepped forward and signaled for the Negroes to push together to open a space on the platform next to Simbatu. "Strip."

"What?" While Joshua questioned the order, two of the other crew stepped down the ladder and circled the two.

"I warned you about making one of these Africans as a pet." He pulled back the lock on his pistol. "Take off your shirt and trousers, and take your place among your fellow slaves, John Manley."

Joshua raised his hands and spread his fingers in rage, just as he had done when Lord Lyddell threatened to kill the brood mare Emily. "Damn your soul to hell, Captain Sperry!" Before Joshua could reach the captain's throat, one of the men hit him on the head with a belaying pin.

An hour later, Joshua woke up naked and shackled on the platform next to Simbatu. "Welcome back, John Manley. How does it feel to be treated like an African?"

"You did this to me!"

"No, Joshua Smoot. You did this thing to yourself when you disobeyed your captain."

"You called my name."

"No—I whispered your name so only you would hear me." The African gave a grunt. "You made the choice to speak to me, and you were told what would happen if you spoke to one of us."

☠ ☠ ☠

The next afternoon, Seaman Parker unshackled Joshua and Simbatu and took them topside. He held two shirts and two pairs of trousers. "Here. Put these on."

"What's happening?"

"We will be dropping the anchor in a few minutes. Get dressed."

"Simbatu is being sent to Baracoa with me?"

"Yes—it is the captain's order."

Joshua turned to the African. "I don't know if this is to be a good thing or a bad thing, but either way, you are right, Simbatu. It is my fault that you are being sold here with me."

With the luffing of her sails, the *Crow* came to a stop in the harbor a hundred yards from the Baracoa waterfront. Captain Sperry walked forward as the last of the slaves were ushered below decks.

"Parker! Are they ready?"

"Aye, Captain!"

"Then get to it."

Parker picked up the first of two hemp ropes. While he made the familiar loop and folded the two halves onto themselves, he stepped to Joshua. "Raise your foot, Manley."

"What are you doing?"

"Unlike you, I am obeying Captain Sperry's order." He slipped the knot around Joshua's ankle and snugged it tight. After doing the same to Simbatu, Parker passed the two ropes over the rail and tied them to the anchor. "There— just like the day I pulled you from the chain locker and gave you that seawater bath."

Joshua turned to Captain Sperry. "You're going to drown us?"

"I'm going to send you to the bottom of this bay. Whether you drown or not will depend on you."

"Are we worth so little to you?"

"Are you begging me for mercy, John Manley?"

"Yes—if that will save our lives."

"But what sort of a message would that give to the rest of my crew?" He looked about at the men who had gathered to watch the spectacle. "All ships captains depend on loyalty from their men, and the way they foster that loyalty varies from one ship to the next. I read a book once that told me that it is better for a leader to be feared than to be loved." He took the time to look at each of his men. "You men are watching me, as you should be." He pointed behind him to Joshua and Simbatu. "If today I let this man and his African pet go without the punishment I warned them they would suffer, every one of you would remember this day and question every order I give from this day forward. Such questioning of my authority always leads to mutiny."

"Isn't selling us here—at Baracoa—punishment enough?"

"No!" He turned back to the two slaves. "You disobeyed my order, John Manley, and for that, you and your African will suffer the harm you brought upon yourself and him."

"I'll take the cat—the stripes both he and I deserve—if it will change your mind."

"You'd do that? You would take his stripes?"

"I did this. I disobeyed your order. Not him."

"A noble gesture, but you are ignoring the way it works between a pet and his master."

"I don't understand."

"A pet always follows his master, and you were warned to never make one of these Africans your pet." He stepped close. "If your African drowns, it is on you, not me."

"All he did was say my name."

"Your hands are free, John Manley. If you can untie those knots before your lungs suck themselves full of sea water, then you will live. If not, then you will die."

One of the sailors called. "Your boat is ready, Captain!"

"Then it's time that we drop anchor." He turned back to Joshua and Simbatu. "I will be waiting to see whether you and your pet survive."

ABOUT THE AUTHOR

Commander Roger L Johnson was born in Los Angeles, California on January 29, 1944. At age nineteen, he was chosen for pilot training at the prestigious Naval Air Training Command where he graduated as the top student from his 57-man class. After three cruises to Vietnam aboard the aircraft carriers Ticonderoga, Enterprise, and Midway, Roger joined the fire service while remaining in the Naval Air Reserves. In 2001, he completed a 28-year career as a Crew Captain with Cal Fire at Klamath, California. Along with his extensive writing endeavors, Roger worked as a cartoonist for three separate magazine publishers. He is now known as the "Turtleman of Gig Harbor," having made and given away nearly a thousand turtles made from stones found on the beach. He and his wife Elizabeth live in Gig Harbor, Washington where he continues to write and create.

Printed in Great Britain
by Amazon